I0573758

"I've been expecting you," said the girl in the gold bathing suit. "Where have you been?"

"Not far, baby, not far," he said, dropping into the sand beside her. "If you were a snake you could have bitten me." He threw himself across her then, and they kissed.

Her hands came from behind her head, hair spilling onto the sand. One hand held him fast about the neck, the other explored, winding down his side, over his thigh. . . .

He began an impatient motion with his hands, but she stopped him.

"Not here," she said. "For this you need time, lots and lots of time. Come down to my apartment tonight. And when you leave you'll wonder where you've been and what you've been doing all these years. I'll own you then. . . ."

The Deadly Desire

Robert Colby

PROLOGUE BOOKS

F + W Media, Inc.

Published in electronic format by
PROLOGUE BOOKS
an imprint of F+W Media, Inc.
10151 Carver Road
Blue Ash, Ohio 45242
www.prologuebooks.com

Copyright © 1959 by Fawcett Publications

All rights reserved.
No part of this publication may be reproduced or transmitted in any form or by any means,
electronic or mechanical, including photocopy, recording, or any information storage or
retrieval system, without permission in writing from the publisher.

eISBN 10: 1-4405-3733-X
eISBN 13: 978-1-4405-3733-2
POD ISBN 10: 1-4405-5800-0
POD ISBN 13: 978-1-4405-5800-9

This is a work of fiction. Names, characters, corporations, institutions, organizations, events,
or locales in this novel are either the product of the author's imagination or, if real, used
fictitiously. The resemblance of any character to actual persons (living or dead) is entirely
coincidental.

This work has been previously published in print format by:
Gold Medal Books, Fawcett Publications, Inc., Greenwich, CT.

FOR MARGARET TAYLOR, MY AUNT,
WITH LOVE

and with gratitude and affection
to the following who helped and
encouraged in the empty time

Alice and Jim Heffernan
Colette Burns
Doris and Bill Siegel
Dorothy Davis
Ethel Loban
Georgia and Vic Robertson
Miriam Purcell
Pauline Stiles
Ruth-Ellen and Clem Storey

PART ONE

one

The name Malibu, California evokes in the
minds of the many who seldom leave the world of their
imaginings thoughts of sweeping, palm-dressed beaches
adorned with bronzed and beautiful movie stars wearing
the perpetual smiles of casual lovers; of sleek yachts at
anchor on a glassy Pacific; of long fast cars and long cool
drinks; and of rich play for idle-rich men and girls dancing
under the spangled heavens on the patios of their lush
beachside homes.

Stanley Royce, who lived in Malibu part of that summer
and who was neither rich nor idle, was reminded of none
of these things when the summer was gone. He did not remember Malibu for its idle rich or its rare glimpses of
movie stars. He tried not to think at all of that month in
August. But when the memory stole upon him, his mind
was like a searchlight peering through a dark tunnel. The
light was a long narrow cone which excluded all but the
one terminal image—so ugly and grotesque that he wished
to destroy the light of his memory so he could never again
look back.

Royce was just thirty that summer. He looked younger
with his flaxen hair, smooth-skinned Nordic clarity of
features, intensely bright blue eyes. He was one who
seemed vaguely out of place here, belonging more to ski
slopes than the cresting hills of Pacific waves.

7

He was a moderately tall man, slim yet broad-shouldered with a looseness about him, a supple strength. Without being too brawny, he seemed a man who could handle himself quickly and decisively in any physical situation.

His face was pleasant and given to frequent smiling in a calm, withdrawn sort of way. He spoke softly and rather deliberately, a look of careful judgment in his eyes. He was thoughtful and generally well liked. He was the sort of person in whom people just naturally confided. They quickly sensed that he was above passing along confidences and idle gossip. He was a man's man who also drew women without the least appearance of trying.

Long before he'd graduated from UCLA, he had become interested in television plays and their direction. Not the club-footed artless plays served from the same tired menu, but sensitive and truthful offerings from gifted writers. He had thought to be a kind of one-man crusade against mediocrity. In this he had been partially successful while gaining experience in the direction of plays produced by Little Theatre. But when he joined an ad agency as an assistant TV producer, he met with the stone wall of conformity to the tried, established patterns of commercialism. The formula was set—never risk a new thoroughbred while the sponsor was selling soap chips with the old gray mare.

However he was patient and moved in company with the progressives. His exacting talent as a director was noted and eventually he was taken in by a newly formed agency. He became the producer of a fine series of one-hour weekly plays written by a quartet of coming playwrights who wrote with the feverish intensity of authors who were angry enough and wise enough to have something to say.

The series was replaced in the summer and, for the month of August, it was his custom to come down from the smoggy hills of Hollywood where he maintained a bachelor apartment and rent a beachside den which looked seaward from that structure known as the Pacific Tides in Malibu.

Royce liked Malibu because while he was outwardly gregarious, he was essentially, and of necessity, a lonely person. And Malibu was essentially a lonely little town, having a basic population of two thousand, though this was doubled and better with the flux of summer visitors. Los

8

Angeles was a good twenty-five miles distant and the near-est city of any size was Santa Monica, some ten miles east on Highway 101.

As for Malibu, it was one of the least commercial beach resorts in its look and feel of solitude. It had only a hand-ful of small stores close by the Sheriff's Station east, and less than a handful in that cluster around Malibu Inn west. Between these points and well beyond, there was nothing much but tight rows of informal dwellings, mostly of the cottage variety; low, rambling apartment houses, motels, gas stations, a few cafes and the Malibu Pier. Most of the movie stars and moguls commanding behind the cameras lived farther west and south of the highway in a section known as The Colony. Their isolation was insured by the necessity of visitors having to pass a guard post before gaining admission to that sacred domain.

Thus a tourist wheeling toward either extreme of San Francisco or San Diego might easily storm through on the coast highway without the remotest idea that Malibu, richly exploited in the journals of the nation, had come and gone.

The Pacific Tides, like the majority of beach apartment houses in the area, was small. It had only six units. There being so few tenants in such close proximity, it was in-evitable that, except for those rare holdouts, the vacationers would soon be on a first-name basis of informality. After all, they shared the same slice of beach and water, same patio and barbecue pit, same car port, meeting each other coming and going at every turn. Sometimes they even tossed gay little parties for themselves in one apartment or another. All very cozy.

It was an arrangement which Royce liked. He could mix with the tenants if he wished, or he could withdraw to catch up on his reading, study the manuscripts of plays for the fall season—or just think. He did much of the latter, while it seemed nearly everyone else hated to think, preferring to drift with The Dream. And this was one of the reasons for his remoteness below the surface. But among comparative strangers he was under no real obliga-tion and he was at liberty to take company or leave it alone. It was his belief that if you were deeply aware and thoughtful, you were bound to be pretty much alone anyway, in company or out.

Because he saw much and understood much of what

9

he saw, was constantly evaluating, Royce had a language of his own beyond idle chatter. And it was foreign. He couldn't use it. He couldn't communicate. And not to communicate was to be alone. So he was constantly looking for someone who spoke the language. That was why he had no really strong friendships. That was why he hadn't married. He was always in search of someone who spoke the language. Perhaps that was why, weary of his professional pals, male and female, he came down from Hollywood each summer to Malibu, unconsciously searching among strangers.

The Pacific Tides was owned by George T. Macklin, a real-estate broker who did not live on the premises but had a cliffside ranch house in the Palisades. Every year Macklin reserved the same apartment for Royce during the month of August. From the very beginning Macklin had assured Royce that the Tides was to be a place primarily for bachelors and young married couples— no children allowed. He was renting only to youthful and "very high-type" tenants. Royce was in some doubt as to their agreement on the definition of high-type, as very often meanings got confused in the minds of landlords to whom a money-type was just naturally a high-type. But Macklin did not seem under any financial pressure and so far Royce had met with people who were quite compatible—and sometimes interesting.

On this, his third summer at the Tides, Royce had no reason to suspect that in choosing his tenants Macklin had brought together such lethal components that hate would smolder and flare—and at last destroy.

two

The apartment building was located beachside along the coast highway about half a mile east of the Malibu Pier and the tiny shopping center. It was a two-story lime green structure of stucco and white wood trim with great masses of window area for capturing the view of the ocean south and the rolling hills and steep cliffs north. A low modern building, it boasted a fine slope of

10

beach, a wide patio, a lawn decked with palms and flowers and a car port for six vehicles. All the rooms were handsomely furnished.

Royce had a second-floor single-bedroom apartment fronting the ocean. As usual upon his arrival, the house was all but full, most of the vacationers having been on hand long enough to become well acquainted if they were so inclined.

It began quietly enough. The first day or two he kept pretty much to himself, reading, baking in the sun, taking an occasional dip in the never-too-warm Pacific. Meanwhile he shuffled the tenants mentally, placing them in the proper apartments, grading their appearances, occasionally saying a few words of greeting. Other times he would just smile or wave, employing all the usual approaches to familiarity.

Macklin was again true to his word. The tenants, if not yet proved "high type," were certainly young enough. Royce hadn't seen but one who looked over thirty-five and the rest were well below. Furthermore, except for a lone married couple, there were only single people. Not a sign of any little free-wheeling brats. As one of the tenants said later, "You can't have any children in most of these god-damn resort houses—they might wake up the late drinkers or peel the wall paint. But what do people do, drown the little bastards?"

It was several days before Royce had edged into conversation with everyone, had all the names committed to memory and stashed away with the right faces. The least sociable of the tenants was the young woman who lived alone in the apartment just below him. She was Star Osborne. And the name was appropriate because in her strange way, she soon became the star attraction.

Royce got his first impression of her when she came out to the beach on his second afternoon, settling down on a blanket just a few yards beyond him. She had chestnut hair, extremely long and brushed so shiny the sun lighted it with tiny glints of fire when she turned her head. She was just above middle stature and a fraction on the plump side, though she had a long, narrow waist and slender legs. Above the waist her breasts were high and taut in the gold bathing suit. The tanned oval of her face had a soft beauty of outline to the round curve of chin. But the cheeks were a little too puffy

11

full, the mouth too wide, a crimson splash across her face. Her structure was a contradiction—slim here, fleshy there. She wouldn't get and didn't need a beauty prize. Royce knew at a glance that her laurels had always been men. For the animal pull of her clung about her. She was lust made visible.

She said nothing to him and he said not a word to her. Oiling her skin with long, busy fingers, falling back to shade her eyes with little patches of cotton, it was as though she were unaware of his presence.

After a bit she seemed to grow restless. She kept changing her position irritably, now sitting, looking out to sea, now reclining again. Then she put on sun glasses and began to read from a pocket novel, swiveling to face the highway. She appeared to read inattentively, her head bobbing up to gaze with a curious intentness at the cars flashing by. Royce could almost feel the pulse of restlessness in her. She seemed a driven creature, tense, nervous. Her drawn face with its pulled-down lips and angry chin screamed of willfulness and impatience.

In five minutes she closed the book, gave a final look to the highway and, standing abruptly, snatched up the blanket and advanced briskly toward the building.

As she approached, her head was held high, her expression withdrawn. Obviously she was going to pass within three feet of Royce without noticing him. Then—suddenly —as she came abreast of his position, she paused, looked down. Her face was without warmth when she announced in a rich husky voice, "My name is Star Osborne." She stood still but seemed already gone in distracted flight.

"Stan Royce," he said flatly, looking up but not smiling. He did not like rude or temperamental people and never gave them ground.

"Well," she said, and there was a flicker of indecision in her wide gray-green eyes. Then she moved off as if she had never spoken, scattering sand with the impatient thrust of her feet.

I'll be god-damned! thought Royce. You meet them all.

His interest aroused, he inquired about her. But to the others she was just a name. She had come nearly a week ago and still no one knew from where or why—or what she was about. And her manner was too forbidding for questions.

12

He saw her several times again but she never spoke. Not until two nights later and then under quite different circumstances.

Meanwhile, by comparison, he found the others easy to know. Giving and taking brief snatches of conversation, he learned the barest essentials of their existence.

With the rear apartments staggered to hold the view, the building ran perpendicular to the beach, probably because in that way it took up less of that premium property. Royce and Star Osborne had the two water-front apartments. Second floor middle was in possession of Rodney "Rod" Lindquist and his wife Muriel. Rod Lindquist was a thin narrow-chested man, pale of face with delicate features and limbs. He was thirty-seven and the oldest. He looked older, perhaps because his light brown hair was sprinkled with premature gray. He spoke with a wryly humorous disdain about nearly everything his conversation touched. He seemed both uninhibited and moody, affable one minute, brusque the next. He was president of a large import-export firm in San Francisco. He drove a new Lincoln Continental but otherwise, in manner and dress, exhibited the casual attitude of one who has long ago found it possible to turn his back to the awesome god of money in the consideration of less tangible problems.

Muriel Lindquist was a young woman who might once have been attractive but had allowed herself to go to fat. The short crop of her dark hair emphasized the round meaty moon of her face. Royce could look at the face, mentally shaving off flesh until he could discern the basic bone structure and find a certain beauty hidden there. The loss of thirty, even twenty pounds would cut away most of her excess. But though she was not bad from the waist up, she had great thighs and hips and a rather absurdly gigantic posterior. Royce figured her for a compulsive eater.

He wondered about the compulsion. Her personality was quiet, indrawn, even shy. She would stand about silently listening to her husband, a wistful kind of worship on her face. Her deep brown eyes following his every movement, she seldom spoke until spoken to, and then in an abstract way, often letting a sentence trail into oblivion.

Below the Lindquists were two bachelors still in their

13

twenties—Jay Humphrey and Bruce Erickson. Jointly they ran a small boat-building concern located inland, somewhere on the outskirts of Inglewood. The boat works had belonged primarily to Humphrey's father, who had fallen to his death from a ladder while painting the wood trim of their second-story home. Unfortunately the ladder was perched over a stone patio. Royce had found this out when he asked Humphrey how he had established his own business at such an early age. Humphrey spoke of his father's death with stoic calm.

Humphrey and Erickson might well have been twins. They looked and acted as if this were the case. Both were tall and also big, wide-shouldered, muscle-thighed, hard of bicep. Both had brush-cut blond hair, though Erickson's was a darker reddish blond, Humphrey's pale, almost white. There was a college-boy sameness in the clean open cut of their sun-darkened faces and especially in their boundless puppy-dog enthusiasm for almost everything. They seemed constantly to be playing at life, though in repose; especially in the eyes of Humphrey, there was a knowing and slightly cynical quality.

There was, of course, a difference in their features. Bruce Erickson had a round heavy face; Humphrey's features were longer and narrower with a suggestion of a Roman nose. In any case, both were handsome specimens.

It was obvious to Royce from the beginning that their friendship was no garden variety. It was an uncommon, immensely close attachment. Behind the jocularity, the teasing and poking and ribbing of each other, the matching of strength in Indian wrestling, the water races and other silly competitions of spirited animals, there was a bond of closeness that Royce would have thought unnatural if he could not read maleness in every fiber of them. The bond was there to be seen in the eyes of one watching the other in unguarded moments of secret pride. It was felt in the aura of togetherness which hung about them.

Once, probingly, when he knew them better, Royce said, "Sure can tell you guys are good buddies, the way you go at it together." Smiling, he added, "If I hung around another joe so much I'd probably wind up clobbering him sooner or later."

Humphrey frowned. There was a faint edge to his voice when he said, "Listen, most people don't know what

14

friendship is. That's because they never went through anything more than a rainstorm together. Bruce and I were non-coms in a line company in Korea. And, brother, that was no rainstorm!"

The last tenant, at least in relation to physical position from beach to highway, was Laura Bishop. She had the back upstairs utility apartment, a combination living room-bedroom with bath and alcove kitchen.

Laura Bishop, as she later admitted, was twenty-six. She had medium-length dark brown hair brushed straight back from the forehead and tied in a knot at the nape of her neck. She was a small, slim girl with sensitive features in which the bone structure was etching-clear. She had good legs, was trim with a rather severe kind of attractiveness. She was almost excessively neat.

She had a look of intelligence, her manner was bright and alert and she was not without warmth. But something in her eyes and the tight lines of her face gave a hint of the ascetic, an indefinable suggestion of austerity.

She taught music appreciation at a private school in The Valley. She was an accomplished pianist and occasionally gave lessons at the small house where she lived with her mother. She never mentioned her father and when Royce inquired of him with only polite interest, she said she hadn't seen him in years and abruptly changed the subject.

She had been ten days at the Pacific Tides, was going to stay the rest of the summer and had come "just to get away for a while." Away from what, Royce could only wonder.

Oddly, in view of her quite sufficient attraction, Laura Bishop remained single.

The sixth unit below Laura Bishop was not really an apartment, just a living room-bedroom with a bath, the north wall forming a backstop for the car port. It had little you could call a view from the single window; there was the noise of the cars coming and going and the necessity of eating out. Altogether it was the least attractive quarter of the Pacific Tides and perhaps for that very reason it remained empty.

Considering the group altogether, Royce decided that there were the ingredients for an interesting, though not necessarily unusual August. However, as always, he was a little disappointed that the interest must be objective

15

since neither of the two unattached females stirred in him any immediate feeling of real warmth or communion. They were seemingly at opposite ends of the pole while his taste lay somewhere in between. No matter, there was much work to be done and he would have peace for the job.

Yet remembering the insolent electrical qualities of Miss Star Osborne, he wondered what would happen if those qualities were unleashed from their frozen insulation of disdain, became exposed as high tension wires whipping in a storm.

He was not long in finding out.

three

She knocked on his door two nights after that first encounter. It was just past eight o'clock. When he opened the door, she was standing there with an oddly loose smile on her face. At first he didn't get it at all. Then he realized she must be a little boozed up.

"Hi, Stan," she said, leaning on the door jamb.

"Something I can do for you, Miss Osborne?" he said coolly, remembering their first meeting.

"I'm bored," she said. "Just wanted to talk. And call me Star. You remember. Twinkle, twinkle?"

"You weren't very talkative last time we met."

"I had things on my mind. C'mon, don't be a wise guy. Let me in."

He stared at her.

"Please . . ."

He stepped aside and let her pass, closing the door. She didn't exactly weave. She walked with a slight list to port. She sank into a chair and crossed her legs, pulling down her skirt with a great show of modesty.

Royce remained standing because he was not sure he wanted to encourage her to stay. There was something about her that made him uneasy.

"Same layout as mine," she said, lighting a cigarette, looking around. "This is better. I like looking down on things."

16

He was silent.

"You don't have a drink around, do you?"

"What would you like?"

"Scotch. You have Scotch?"

He shook his head. "I have bourbon. And vodka. Do you really think you need anything at all?"

She squinted up at him, her face set in determined lines. She seemed to measure him from behind the smoke screen of her cigarette. She saw something that changed her expression from a demand to a pouting plea.

"Of course I'm a little loaded," she said. "But I can handle it. Bourbon and just a—" she separated thumb and forefinger a fraction—"just a that-much of soda." She smiled in a way that said, You can't refuse if I put it so nicely.

He nodded. "A yard of bourbon and an inch of soda." He went to the kitchen and made a drink that was almost the other way round, hesitated, then made himself one, too. What the hell. He might as well get her number right from the start. And no better time than when she was a little high.

He set the drink on a table beside her and sat down with his own, lighting a cigarette. From an open window came the hollow liquid sigh of the surf.

"Been here long?" he said.

"Oh, no. Less than a week." She took a sip of her drink, made a face. "No muscle at all," she said. "You'll never make a bartender."

"Less than a week?" he repeated.

"Yes. When I first came, all they had was that stuffy little room in the back. I stayed there because the owner told me he had a cancellation and I could have the front apartment in a few days."

"You're from out of town?"

"Uh-huh. Cleveland."

"Quite a distance. What brings you so far?"

She sighed. "Boredom. It's like a needle. Keeps jabbing me along. Anyway, I always wanted to see good old Malibu—sin and salt water, movie stars, glamor. God! And then when my husband died, I—well, I—" Her voice trailed.

"I'm sorry," he said. But they were just words. He couldn't feel anything for her.

"You're sorry," she said. "Are you really now?" She

got up with the drink and crossed to the window, looked down. "Well, don't be." She turned. "It's just an act with me. People expect it. He was a bastard. Grade A, number one. I hated him."

"Oh?"

"He had nothing good for me. Only money." She snickered. "Lots and lots of money. But he drank too much. Way too much. And familiarity breeds—contagion. I caught the habit."

"Well, now that he's gone," said Royce, "you can break it."

She came across the room toward him and suddenly he was sure she wore no bra under the yellow sweater. It was a difficult thing to tell because her breasts hadn't the least sag.

She leaned over him a little unsteadily, her drink tilted in one hand, the long spill of her hair so close to his face he could detect what he thought was a faint smell of gardenia. Surprising how perfume in subtle measure excites, suggests. And why should it really?

"You're so damn contained," she said. "I hate people who are contained. It makes me want to uncontain them. Uncontain—or attain. I don't know which I mean. What is it with you? A smug quality?"

"Look, Osborne," he said. "Are you just hunting for someone to fight? Because if you are, if drinking brings out all your cute belligerence, take the gloves with you and go set up the ropes right down in your own little den."

The truth was that his coldness was a defense. He knew that. She was spoiled and willful and . . . something else, he didn't quite want to think about. He didn't like her. And yet, in spite of this, if he didn't watch himself, he was going to get involved with her. My God, he didn't have the stone's resistance to a magnet. But if he got involved with her it would be a sour-sweet, soiled attraction. She would have a quicksand pull on him. He could feel it. And he wanted this month to be free of that sensual bog which muddies the mind. He wanted to be thoughtful and objective.

She was laughing. "I like you," she said between spasms, then grew serious. "You've got steel coils for guts running around inside you, Stanley. You've got a way with women, especially my kind."

18

"What is your kind, Osborne?" His head was back and she was leaning over him, and out of the cream-in-coffee tan, the mocha richness of her skin, stretched the red open wound of her mouth, lips back from fine even teeth, moist from the pink dart of her tongue, a small stain of lipstick marring the enamel whiteness of one gleaming tooth.

"My kind? That's something you'll have to find out for yourself, Stanley. And the way you're going at it, you will. If you want to get rid of me, Stanley, you've got the wrong approach. For that you would have to be nice to me like the others—sweet, sweet, sweet. Too much sweetness makes me sick, sick, sick, Stanley."

"For Christ's sake, stop calling me Stanley. And while you're at it, move back and give me drinking room, will you?"

He really didn't want her to go at all. But she kept irritating one side of him and stimulating the other.

She stood and looked at him with a down-twist of smile. "Thatta boy, Stan. You see, I'm calling you Stan and I'm humble and obedient and I'm going back now and sit in my little chair and you're still on the right track, mister. Mister Stan, sir."

Now her smile was quite charming as she fell into her chair, sipping her drink with a little-girl pensiveness. And in spite of himself, he was smiling, too.

"You have a nice smile," she said. "It creeps up on you like wine. But you're stingy with it. Got any canned music? A radio, even?"

"A radio," he said, and crossing the room, dialed in a heavy classic to goad her.

"My hair is long, but not that long," she said.

He changed the station.

"You look like good dancing," she said.

He shrugged and they danced.

After that she remained pleasant, a complete reverse of herself. And forgetting his resolution, the irritation left him and he began to match her, drink for drink. She had built an immunity for she remained at the same level of intoxication while he caught up with her.

She would not reveal more about herself, so he told her of his work and she made intelligent comments. They danced in silence. The startling effect of her against him sealed his speech.

19

Around eleven she stretched, said, "Well, guess I'd better take the ladder and go below, mate. Or would you like me to stay?"

He looked at her. Did she mean— They hadn't even kissed. "You'll have to translate that," he said. "Stay means ten minutes or an hour or—"

"All night," she finished. "Which would you prefer?"

"Which do you offer?"

"I offer nothing. I simply take. And I have all night for that."

"I don't know," he said. He really didn't. Again he was uneasy and didn't quite understand why.

"Reluctance is intriguing," she said. Once more she was bending over him. But this time her lips drew closer, then spread over his mouth. He grabbed her and pulled her down. He fell into a vortex of desire. The want of her was brutally insistent.

She stood. "Well then, if that's your answer, darling . . ." Slowly she eased the sweater upward over a cream expanse of flesh.

Out of his stupor came a nudge of warning. What in God's name is wrong with me? he asked himself, as seeing his uncertainty she delayed with the sweater. I want this bitch, whatever she is. And yet . . . "What the hell," he said aloud, and flipped open the first button of his shirt. He was just drunk enough not to care.

She was laughing at him. "You're sure now," she said. "Don't make any mistakes. Don't reach for that next button unless you mean it. Because, darling," she murmured, "you're going to be lost for a long time." She caressed her body. "You may never find your way out of these woods."

"Shut up," he said softly.

He gave his shirt a violent wrench that took away all the buttons. And, as he did this, she pulled the sweater over her head and stood smiling at him as her fingers worked with the skirt.

Watching, he knew then why he had delayed. He could see in her what he had first felt that day on the beach. He had been right. The animal pull clung about her. She *was* lust made visible. She seemed not so much a woman as a consuming force. And while this had merely disturbed him then, it was almost frightening now.

Even so, he was getting up and fumbling with his belt.

And she was standing there naked—laughing obscenely.

20

When Stan Royce awoke in the morning, she was gone. It was ten minutes before eleven and there was a bright burst of sunlight in the room. It seemed unreal to him that she had been there at all—the fragment of a confused dream, heavy with a degrading and perverted taint of sensuality. Unreal until he saw the smear of lipstick on the second pillow of his double bed, caught the scent of a perfume once suggestive, now sickeningly sweet against the brackish purity of the air from his window.

His lips felt swollen, his mouth parched, unpleasant tasting, denying the pleasures of too much alcohol and too much oral intimacy. There was the vague pulsing throb of a headache. He saw with some annoyance, for he was generally fastidious, the disorder of his clothing on a chair, the whisky bottle on the night table, glasses with the amber dregs of stale liquor and an ashtray spilling with too many butts.

Yawning, he climbed out of bed, covered his nakedness with the terry-cloth robe and stumbled into the kitchen. He measured water and coffee into a pot and set it to boil, squeezed a glass of orange juice, bringing it with him to the bathroom.

Precisely, deliberately, he went about the details of shaving, brushing his teeth, taking a shower, combing his hair, dressing. The whole god-damn ritual was a bore. Every day the same repetition until you died.

When it was all done, he stood at a window, munching toast, sipping his coffee. The ocean looked calm in the distance, but inshore the jade water rolled itself lazily into steep cliffs, tumbled down and raced in a white avalanche toward the beach, then receded into oblivion, to begin the process all over again. . . .

Well, at least she had been gone when he awoke. He was glad. That made it less complicated, not so messy, not so real.

Damn it to hell! Why did he make anything of it? She wasn't the first dame who had crept in and out of his

21

bed, leaving only the suggestion of a bad taste. And most had been forgotten for more important things a few minutes after he opened his eyes.

Then why did she linger in his mind with a haunting unpleasantness?

It didn't take long to figure that one out. Her love-making was not the simple gratification of an animal need. It was the protracted orgy of a limitless appetite. If last night was typical, her lovers were not so much partners as victims. Like the vampire, and with the same stealthy cunning, she robbed them for her needs. And left them enervated physically and soiled spiritually. For in the manner of her love-making there was something too bent and skillful, too hypnotically debased for mundane understanding. It was like an exotic opiate so habit-forming that once it gained dominion, there was no release.

Yet, in another sense, it was ridiculous. For she was one to be desired by all men in search of the sobbing heights of sensual ecstasy. She was a prize beyond the knowledge and imagination of most. And since Royce was far from being a sexual prude, had more than his share of physical drive, he should now consider that he had fallen willy-nilly upon a Pandora's Box of priceless delights. Indeed, this was exactly how he felt. But only in part. For there was a stronger side of him which would not give itself to anything that left him without the power of full and immediate control. He was moderate in all things physical and lived more with his mentality than his body. And he was certain of a reverse situation if he allowed himself another experience with Star Osborne. She would possess him in such an unwholesome way that she might weaken his individuality. And that was a price he was not willing to pay.

So in the end, he decided that the best way not to form a habit was to leave the drug entirely alone. No thank you, he would have no more Osborne. Quietly, without fanfare, he would make this exceedingly plain to her. And that would be the end of it. He was just a little proud in thinking that most men would not be able to accomplish this feat of control, let alone desire it.

Satisfied, but by no means elated with his decision, he went out to the beach to see what else the day had to offer besides the magnetic and perfumed evil of Star Osborne.

Laura Bishop was there on the sand. She lay prone on a candy-striped beach robe. Her white bathing suit emphasized the deep black of her hair, the sun-darkening of her skin. At her elbows there was a pocket-sized portable radio from which eddied faintly the strains of some indistinguishable melody. Her head was raised slightly, chin cupped in the palm of one hand, the other holding sun glasses. She chewed on one stem of the glasses as she watched with a half-smile and squinting interest the movements of Jay Humphrey and Bruce Erickson. These two were preparing to launch their sixteen-foot boat into the surf, loading it with oars and fishing tackle, including a cruel-looking, long-shafted harpoon, a gaff, rods and other paraphernalia. At the moment, they were checking the gas supply in one of the bright red tanks and had not yet mounted the eighteen-horse Evinrude at the stern.

Royce observed that it was a trim little green boat, sleek and sturdy, though apparently light. It had a nice flare at the bow, good freeboard and beam for a small craft, a solid transom to sustain the weight of a heavy motor.

Humphrey and Erickson had brought the boat with them on a trailer and kept it beneath the overhang of Star Osborne's seaview balcony, which projected above the beach. Even at high tide the water wouldn't rise that far, though as a precaution they had the boat tied to a beam. It was also covered with a tarp to keep moisture from the interior. Each day when the pair brought the boat in they cleaned it lovingly, storing the outboard motor in a compartment next to the car port.

Royce sauntered over to inspect the boat closely. Both men wore faded green coveralls and identical yachting caps. Erickson was bent above one of the two portable gas tanks, peering at the gauge. Humphrey stood looking out to sea, hands on hips.

"Sweet-looking design," said Royce to Humphrey. "One of your own?"

"Sure thing," said Humphrey with a toothy grin of pride. "We have a smaller job, fourteen feet, and an eighteen-footer. But I like this one best—fast and dependable. She'll ride dry in some pretty tough water. Even so, fill 'er up like a bath tub and she won't sink."

"Is that so? Won't sink?"

"Nah. Look there, under the seat. Flotation tanks.

23

Long as you don't punch holes in those, she'll stay up forever. As a test we sank 'er to the gunnels in a swimming pool, let half a dozen people swarm all over 'er, and she wouldn't go down."

"Good sales point," said Royce. "I notice you use an eighteen horse. Won't she take more?"

"Sure. She'll take a thirty-five. Look at the beef in that transom. But that's a lot of motor to be lugging around and it's too heavy to fool with through this surf. Boat's too sluggish until you can get up power."

"I wouldn't want to launch in that surf today," said Royce. "You guys have guts."

"It doesn't take guts," said Erickson, kicking the tank lightly with the toe of his sneakered foot, giving his brush-cut a quick fluff with one big hand. "You just have to be a god-damn fool, like Jay, here. I only go along to see he doesn't get into trouble."

Humphrey gave him a hard, playful poke which he took on the blade of his shoulder without flinching or giving ground.

"Don't pay any attention to my father," said Humphrey. "Old dad is cautious, you know. Actually, going through this surf is like anything else that looks dangerous. You've got to know how. Takes good timing and a little skill, that's all."

At that moment Royce had an eye-corner glimpse of Laura Bishop. She was watching Humphrey intently, approvingly, and with a wistful air of speculation. There was already the beginning of something between them. It must have been underway before Royce came. He had seen them sprawled together head-to-head on the beach only yesterday. Humphrey did not notice that she was watching him.

Of the two, it seemed to Royce that Humphrey was the mature, the dominant one. He exuded confidence and strength. The force of his ego was tempered by an impression of amiable forthrightness. Yet Humphrey also seemed shrewd and there was about him the barest hint of self-concealment.

"Well, it's a fine boat," said Royce. "Must be a good seller. I should think you fellows would be on vacation at just the wrong time. Isn't the summer your best season for sales?"

"That's right," said Humphrey. "But you can't sell what you haven't got."

"I don't follow," said Royce.

"He means," said Erickson with boyish pride, "we're at saturation."

"Our line is moving so fast," said Humphrey, "we're still working on back orders. It isn't a matter of having a lot of stock on hand we have to get out and push. Seller's market. At least right now." His smile held a shading of condescension. "What better time for a vacation, wouldn't you say, Royce?"

"I'd say," Royce answered quietly.

"C'mon," said Erickson. "Get the lead out. We need more gas for this buggy."

"No hurry," said Humphrey. It was a rebuke.

"Where you headed?" said Royce.

"We'll take a run over to Paradise Cove," replied Humphrey. "Lot of blue shark there on the surface. You can count the fins. We might stab a couple for kicks. Maybe next time you'd like to go along."

"Sure," said Royce. "Any time. Well, then—" He turned to leave.

Humphrey caught his arm. "How do you like the Star gazing?" he asked.

"Pardon?"

"I mean the Star with the curves, not the points," said Humphrey with a sly smile.

"She's beautiful, don't you think?" said Erickson reverently.

"Star Osborne, you mean," said Royce. "Of course." He forced a smile. Did they know? Had they been watching? He studied their faces. Nothing revealed but Erickson's worship and Humphrey's lusty smile of approval. "Well," he said ambiguously, "she's a lot of woman. Anyone can see that . . ."

"You don't have to see it," said Humphrey, turning toward her apartment meaningfully, "you can feel it. Christ! It's in the god-damn air."

"Jesus," said Erickson in a hushed, awed tone. "If she didn't act like she belonged to someone, I'd—"

"She belongs to me and I'm not selling," said Humphrey.

"You can't sell what you haven't got, remember?" Erickson teased.

25

"We'll see about that," said Humphrey.

"She hasn't shown any signs of being friendly up till now," said Erickson. "Besides, you've got your little bundle. Don't hog it all."

"What bundle?"

Erickson inclined his head slightly toward Laura Bishop.

"Her? Nice, but cool, man. You can't live in a deep freeze all the time."

"They're all cool until you break them down," said Erickson. "Patience. You got to stalk the game through a whole god-damn jungle of words first, man."

"You know anything about her—the Osborne dame?" said Humphrey, turning to Royce. "What gives with her? Where does she come from?"

"Not much I can tell you," said Royce with a fair degree of honesty.

"You haven't staked a claim?"

Royce looked at him and couldn't tell. "No claim," he said. "Open territory."

"Thanks," said Humphrey.

"For nothing," said Royce.

Erickson seemed left out and brooding.

"Don't forget about the ride," said Humphrey. "Next time, Royce, okay?"

"Sure," said Royce.

He departed with a small salute. He and Laura Bishop exchanged pleasant smiles and he walked off down the beach.

five

She must have been spying from the window because she came striding along in her gold bathing suit to meet him. He had walked almost to the long thrust of the Malibu Pier spilling itself into the ocean holding bent blobs of ragged-looking people indolently fishing under the high glare of sun. He had come halfway back and was watching some boys adjusting the sails of a graceful catamaran when she approached with a twist of possessive

26

smile which denied nothing of the night before. There was a savage, dynamic quality in the roving-over-him of her eyes, the willful push of her chin. Seeing her, he felt a twinge of distaste arguing against a latent bloom of desire.

"No bathing suit, darling?" she said. "It's positively unwholesome to go about dressed on such a day."

"I don't feel wholesome." He began to walk and she fell in beside him. "I didn't know the word was in your vocabulary."

"Nice try, Stanley. But you don't have to insult me today. After last night, I'm completely won over."

"Last night was last night," he said. "Consider it as an isolated incident."

"Maybe you don't feel like the beach, darling. A change would be good for you. All those beautiful hills up there looking down on the little people. We could take a blanket and some sandwiches and a thermos full of—what? Martinis? And a couple of good books to read. Or maybe we wouldn't need the books." Chuckling. "And we could have a regular picnic, just the two of us."

He could picture it. Between the lines she made it visual. Under the naked sun, the naked bodies entwined, the wet embrace in the dry air with the grassy, woodsy smells attending. The slow dragging on cigarettes, relaxed after the spent pleasure, supine on the blanket, the mind vapid of its jagged content, at rest. Another Martini, darling? How about a sandwich? Oh, he could picture it, desire it—almost need it. In the memory of last night the urge was demanding. With someone else he might have gone gladly. With someone else it would end there. Or go on for a space without compulsion. But this one wanted to absorb him, use him up. And if there was an end at all, it would be in some final degradation, the essence of which he could already feel.

"I never cared much for picnics," he said. "Besides, I have some work to do. One of the reasons I came here was to jell some ideas I have, get them down on paper. Quietly. And alone."

"Stanley. You're avoiding me, Stanley."

"Yes, I suppose I am."

"You know, Stanley, I've let a lot of men drown in their own little graves of unrequited tears. But I've never had a man drop me after he had his bliss. It would be a

27

new experience for me, Stanley. I wouldn't like it. Not at all."

He paused, swung her around to face him. "Listen, don't give me any of those cute little veiled threats. Big bad men don't scare me, let alone neurotic little girls with prize-winning chests. Why, for God's sake, we hardly know each other. One night together and you act like you own me."

"But what a night, darling. And how lightly you take it."

"It was offered lightly and I took it lightly."

"Don't fool yourself, Stanley. I'm perfectly serious and always was. I never start anything I don't want to finish. I told you to be careful and think twice—remember? Never mind, I'll sew the buttons back on. But that won't change a thing."

"All right," he said. "That's enough. That's plenty. This is just the kind of muck I don't want. Clear? So go on and get lost before I say something you wouldn't want to hear."

"That's all?" she said. There was real hatred in her eyes, out of all proportion. It puzzled and worried him.

"That's all," he said.

"Very well," she said softly and with the trace of an evil smile. "I have patience. I'll wait. Meanwhile I'll be busy, Stanley. I'm going to be exceedingly busy."

"I'll bet," he said.

But she was gone, kicking sand up the beach.

six

Laura Bishop saw the young woman called Star Osborne pushing swiftly through the sand toward the apartment house. The Osborne girl's face was set in angry lines, her head uptilted so that the cords of her neck stood out, ugly with strain, malice even in the quick march of her steps.

As Laura watched with mixed emotions—she didn't like that one, but was intensely curious—Star Osborne flounced by her without so much as a down-glance of acknowledgement. This was only a minor source of irritation since the woman was obviously in a state and had

28

never said one word to Laura in the first place.

But now, as she was about to enter her apartment, Star Osborne paused on the steps and looked over to where Jay Humphrey and Bruce Erickson were just that moment setting gas tanks in the boat and fastening some rubber hoses that looked like little black snakes to the motor. They were obviously about ready to leave and Laura was sure Jay was going to ask her along because he had mentioned taking her just yesterday.

In truth, she really didn't want to go. At least, she wanted to go very badly because it would be so nice to be near Jay for another few hours, but on the other hand she was a little frightened. The waves roll d so high sometimes, like today, building those big green walls that came smashing down with a look of such heedless and brutal power. She could just see the little boat swing broadside, curling under the lip of a giant comber, spinning over and over and down in slow motion, sucked under, a toy boat with toy people, all crushed and swallowed in tons of water.

But she had told Jay she would just *love* to go. And she was perfectly sincere—that is, after they got out beyond the breakers it would be a glorious adventure. Glorious! And of course the real glory would be in the nearness to that rugged, that lithe and graceful, that guilelessly handsome man—Jay Humphrey. Such a clean openness about him. Clean, clean . . .

Yet now as she watched with a horrible sort of fascination, that Star Osborne's whole expression began to change, exactly like some Jekyll and Hyde transformation. She was absolutely rooted on the steps, her head turned toward the boat, watching, her face muscles suddenly relaxed and a thin smile nudging at the corners of those dreadfully overblown and cheaply sensual lips.

Laura could read her mind as though her thoughts had formed into words which were engraved on her forehead in big block letters. Laura could feel her own muscles bunching to rise. There was still time, the boys hadn't noticed and Star Osborne was granite-still—a statue, poised. Yet Laura had pride and she had purposely avoided going over to the boat and standing around, an unspoken demand which couldn't be decently refused. And now she wasn't going to be caught in a silly race of females for The Prize. Singular, because while she

29

liked Bruce Erickson a whole lot, another nice clean boy, he was rather juvenile at times and stirred nothing in her but a kind of mothering tenderness, the way she felt about an occasional pupil in her classes. Not the same thing at all.

Anyway, it was too late. As she expected, Star Osborne finally came to life. Moving just as languidly as she had moved tensely seconds before, she came back down the steps and over to the boat, walking with a certain slow undulating grace, her expression innocent now—little-girl-curious.

They were too far removed for Laura to hear what was said, but it wasn't difficult to imagine. A pretense of complete and sole interest in the boat, followed by clever little exchanges of slightly suggestive banter, the body-beautiful posing in various attitudes of display all the while. How odd, as not once that Laura could remember had the Osborne girl shown a flicker of interest since her arrival.

Though she was not usually given to secret resentments of her competition, this was just the type female person Laura detested. The Star Osbornes of the world—if there was ever one quite like her, for she had a frighteningly bestial quality—were awful frauds. Awful! Selfish beyond comparison. Dirty beyond comprehension to clean minds. They displayed a surface and completely simulated interest in the sports, ambitions and intellectual pursuits of a man while teasing his base instincts with every glance, smile and posture. And if she had a certain gaudy attraction, the man rationalized himself right into the trap. Nice women simply loathed this sort. And not because they were jealous or afraid of competition.

Looking at Jay Humphrey standing tall and clean but nevertheless head bent over Star Osborne in such a way that while they talked he must be gazing right down the top of her bathing suit, Laura was reminded of Lee Bricknell. Married now, three children. Married to a girl who got him with the same deceitful tactics of Star Osborne.

Lee Bricknell. He had looked and acted so much like Jay that it was painful. Or was this an illusion of time and was it more that Jay and Lee had the same outdoor purity of line, the scrubbed-looking exterior, perenially youthful? And the same unspoiled mentality with its

30

simple directness; a kind of honesty of spirit which had not yet gone sour from the insidious rot which was drawn by osmosis from a cynical, sordid world.

Perhaps, though, thought Laura, she merely saw these things because she wanted to. For didn't she know, couldn't she learn that innocent faces and innocent words could hide dark tides beneath?

Well, Lee Bricknell was dead. Love-dead, a soggy thing inside her. She squeezed her eyes tight and drew the shades of her mind against thinking about him or picturing him. Over. Gone. It wasn't her fault. She couldn't help the way she was. She didn't know that was what he wanted until too late, the sex thing which someone else had given him, the dirty thing they all wanted in secret, underneath the pretty words and the pretty smiles.

Did Jay want that as Lee had, even before . . . ? He didn't seem to, Jay didn't. "Of course I understand, Laura." Parked in his car up there on the hill, the third night in a row. "I'm only human, but it's not just sex with you. You're too sweet, too good, Laura. It's just a way of showing my affection. There, now, don't cry. You're a little frozen and clutched inside yourself with fear. You need someone to understand you, Laura honey. And I'm the one. You'll see. You need a different kind of love, right? Sure, sure. Cigarette? No? Well, shall we go back now . . . ?"

At that moment she was sure that she loved him even more than she had ever loved Lee Bricknell. Perhaps it was his patience and understanding of her need. And yet, beneath this patience and understanding she sensed the male aggression moving strongly toward its goal. And was the more attracted—and at the same time repulsed.

Maybe it was her mother with that icy disdain for men, the little remarks about their disgusting and filthy obsession with, not sex—the word was never mentioned—but "carnal passion." Of course, her mother was bitter, her father having gone down to the drugstore one night when Laura was ten, and never coming back, just disappearing, swallowed by the darkness as though he never existed. And that Langley woman, the widow next door, packed and gone the day before so that you had to put two and two together.

Still, there was a rightness in what her mother said. She was pious, a completely devoted Southern Baptist,

31

and her words had a way of becoming absorbed through the years, worn like an inner cloak of protection. But now perhaps it was time she moved out on her own. Because even if her mother wasn't ever going to get married again . . . No, it was really a little abnormal, this living together in a small apartment and she would have to think about it seriously. Her mother wasn't holding her, wasn't trying in the least to keep her from her own life. Not in the least.

Anyway, all men liked her—at first. Some came back a second and third time. Occasionally she had a continuing association which lasted a month or two—in a rather palsy way. But in the end, even the palsy ones, the confessors of affairs with other women, faded and were gone. Didn't they understand that it wasn't because she wasn't perfectly normal—perfectly! But that all her instincts were washed and decent and, well, pure. Such a grim, sanctimonious word. But it was true. And after she was married, they would see how willing and—ha!—carnally passionate she could be.

In her mind, at least, she felt as if she could be ungovernably passionate with Jay Humphrey. Because she loved him in all other ways, though he didn't know it. And that's what made her cry up on the hill. Because she couldn't—just couldn't—beyond the quick, dry kiss. But later, if he would wait, if it ever got around to marriage . . . Yes, maybe he would be the one to wait. He had to be the one! Something was convulsing inside her, screaming for him to be The One.

But now they were pushing the boat into the surf, Jay not once looking back but helping Star Osborne into the stern, pushing, pushing, faster, faster. Now Jay and Bruce had hopped in and Bruce was rowing madly in the lull between waves, trying to make it out there before the first big one came pitching in, folding over them. It didn't look good. There was a space and then a high sweep, a green monster of water humping up for the fall. They weren't going to make it!

I hope they don't! I hope they don't! I hope that wave drives them right down to the bottom. Especially her! No, I didn't mean it. No! Please God, let them get through.

There! The little boat rose, climbed, peered over the top and slid down the other side to safety. Indistinctly

32

she could see their faces. They were all laughing—a big joke.

Now she could hear the motor, saw them leap ahead, piling foam like snowdrifts at the bow. Bruce was up there at the wheel. And at the stern, the gold bathing suit with a stripe of green around the back that was Jay Humphrey's arm.

Lost, she thought. Lost. He's lost. No. Maybe not. But she would have to change—suddenly. Revoltingly. She bit down hard on the shell stem of the glasses. She would have to change to get him, be like the others. Or Star Osborne would devour him. And all the time she wanted everything to be so clean, clean, clean.

seven

The little boat was circling beyond the breakers, waiting for the precise moment when it could be slammed up the beach without swamping. Erickson was at the wheel and Humphrey sat astern with Star, both leaning back luxuriously, his arm about her waist. It had been a beautiful voyage, and Erickson had made good use of the passing hours.

Laura Bishop had disappeared indoors as the boat rounded the Malibu Pier, a small cloud of disturbance on her face. But Rod and Muriel Lindquist were watching from their position on a blanket perched in front of the building. Both were in bathing suits, Muriel with her absurd bowling-pin kind of shape crowding the lower extremes of the suit. Rod, in contrast, appeared more delicate and slim than ever, his pale skin resisting the sun inexorably, except for an occasional patch of pink trying for a tan and never quite making it.

Now the green boat found a smaller wave in the series and came roaring in full throttle just behind it, following the foaming breakage with neat timing, Humphrey hoisting up the motor stem at the last moment so the prop wouldn't dig sand, doing this when Erickson cut throttle, the boat carried by momentum almost to dry beach.

Erickson jumped first from the bow, Humphrey right behind. Star remained poised astern, the queen-bee pleased

33

and smug as she was hauled ashore by the sweating drones.

Muriel stayed squat and placid on the blanket, but Rod Lindquist had seen the flip of a tail fin and went down with Royce to inspect.

"Shark, isn't it?" said Rod with a faint look of disapproval.

"A blue," said Humphrey, passing a smile back and forth between Rod and Star who was just now climbing from the boat with a fine display of bosom. "About six feet, wouldn't you say, Rod?"

"Six feet of nothing," said Rod scowling. "Why bother to bring a thing like that in? Just stink up the god-damn place."

The shark lay belly up on the deck, tail fin resting on a corner of the after-seat. The jaws were open, half-moon mouth below the long snout revealing the slant of jagged teeth. The white belly was smeared with blood and from beneath the head more blood had oozed onto the deck. Even in death, the fish had a look of sleek malevolence.

"Star wanted her picture taken, then we'll drag it off and bury it," said Erickson.

"Did she catch it?" asked Lindquist, directing the question to Humphrey.

"I helped reel it in, Mr. Lindquist," Star said. "Then Jay speared it with this." She reached in the boat and held up the long oak shaft and dart of a harpoon—vicious metal, bloodstained.

Royce stepped closer and examined the harpoon. The head was of a type called a butterfly dart. It was of heavy brass and sharply pointed with spread wings. It could be hurled or thrust deeply into the body of a fish, the winged barbs holding it fast in the meat. A simple weapon, but deadly efficient.

Rod Lindquist turned to Star, said, "So you want your picture taken." He dropped his eyes to the shark. "Well, you both have nice teeth."

He was smiling, but at that moment Royce was sure Lindquist didn't like her.

Unperturbed, she turned away from him, supporting herself with a hand on Humphrey's mass of shoulder. "Hi, Stan," she said. "Having fun, boy?"

Her face was bland, even pleasant. Another reversal.

34

She had stopped hating him suddenly—or never did. Royce couldn't understand her. The real motivation behind all her actions was completely obscure. "Fun?" he said. "That depends. We all have our own definition."

"We'll have to get together sometime and discuss terminology," she replied.

Rod Lindquist watched and listened. On his pale face there was about the same expression of distaste with which a minute ago he had viewed the shark.

"I never could get excited about a damn slimy fish," he said. "I never ate more than a bite of one and never went fishing in my life." He chuckled. "I suppose if there's any eating to do, this one would do it. You hear all kinds of stories. Is this type dangerous?"

"Well—" said Humphrey.

"Some sharks are harmless," interrupted Erickson. "Like the sand shark and the basking shark. But the blue shark is man-eating." He spoke as from rote, his eyes rolling sideways to Star and back to Lindquist who nodded solemnly and glanced at the shark with still more repugnance.

"Well," continued Humphrey, "it's not that they're so dangerous. They're just stupid. Every once in a great while they see a hunk of man-meat swimming around and they think it's another fish and instead of asking questions they go tearing in and take a good bite for themselves. They're completely lacking in judgment or the finer instincts."

Laughter.

"They're tough bastards, though," said Humphrey, warming to his audience. "I wouldn't want to boat one until he's very dead. They won't hold still to be clubbed and when you do get to beat hell out of them, they get mad because it tickles. So what we do is to troll around until one picks up the bait, then reel him in and spear him with this harpoon we call a lily iron. But that just irritates him, doesn't kill him. So we let him take this dart which detaches from the shaft and go swim off with it. But, being tricky buggers, we have a rope tied to the dart and at the other end of the rope is a fat little keg. Mr. Blue sounds, pulls the keg down until he tires, gives up and dies. Simple. C'mon, Bruce, we'll flip him over and let them have a look."

Together they got the shark turned to. "See what I

35

mean?" said Humphrey. "You'd think a wound like that would kill him."

Just back of the head there was an ugly gutted crater and a loose flapping of skin where the dart had been removed.

"What a sweet picture that will make," said Lindquist.

"We'll show him the other way, underbelly front," said Bruce Erickson. "Toss a gaff into him, Jay, so we can carry him. I'll run up and get my camera."

"He's so cute about it all," said Star to Erickson's back, receding up the beach. "Perfectly darling!"

"Perfectly," said Lindquist.

eight

From above on the blanket, Muriel Lindquist watched the excitement over the shark without much interest. She knew her husband detested fish, especially bruised and bloody ones, even more than she did. So it must be that woman in her gaudy bathing suit which somehow managed to be at least a size too small so that her breasts were about half exposed all the time. Of course it was true that she had—what would the men call it?— a luscious figure. Simply luscious. And pretty hair and that big mouth . . . Yes, she was quite a package and Muriel would be fair enough and just objective enough to admit that there was a naked kind of appeal about her. Naked. That was the only word you could use because she flaunted, simply flaunted herself in a manner that would leave her completely unclothed in a fur coat. Even if she had the desire to make that kind of a spectacle, what other woman would have the nerve?

Muriel was just a little envious of that nerve. There had been a time not so long ago when she wasn't, well, as—plump—as she was now. And then she had been quite handsome and she was provoked by the sneaky affair she knew Rod was having into thinking it would be fun to flirt. But she never had the nerve. And anyway, when she would try to strike a compelling and naughty pose in front of her mirror, just practicing, the image she saw reflected was so ridiculous it only made

36

her laugh. Not because she wasn't attractive enough for seduction—heavens, no—but because her eyes, her whole expression gave the lie to such posturing. No matter what she did she always looked so mild. And, of course, she was, really. Mild and shy with anyone but Rod and full of deep thoughts she was unable to express to anyone but Rod. And not him always, either. No, because they weren't as close as they used to be.

The odd part of it was that she had always been so sure Rod loved her, even though their marriage wasn't built on any great physical passion. Heavens, that passion business couldn't sustain a marriage anyway, even if it lasted past the first year, the passion. And Rod had never seemed abundantly interested in sex. He just wasn't a physical type, like that Humphrey man who simply exuded sensuality in his deceptively wholesome, nature-boy manner. No, on the contrary, Rod was kind of passive about it all. That is, until he got involved with that woman at the office, that Andrea Tedesco who had been his secretary while the other girl was out sick.

Muriel might never have known. She hadn't met Miss Tedesco and Rod only mentioned her casually. It didn't enter her mind. Rod had never shown real interest in another woman or cheated to her knowledge. In fact, when Rod found reasons to be away from home two or three nights a week, she still wasn't suspicious. Her hunch was born when he became a little too attentive, when he lost some of that gruff exterior with which he covered his affection and especially when she saw he was troubled about something and trying to conceal it. Rod didn't conceal trouble. Sooner or later he always talked it out with her, explaining, seeking advice, or if she had none, just using her as a vent. In this facet of his personality alone, there had been a basis for a special understanding between them.

But suddenly he was disturbed and wouldn't admit it. Disturbed while the outlook was so bright—business good, more money than they could spend. Twelve-room house, two cars, two servants and a nurse for sweet little Julie, their six-year-old, everyone in good health, the horizon unblemished. And Muriel knew if there was some problem about money or health or business, or even a personal rift, he would not be able to contain it. He would seek her out. But since he was troubled and was killing himself hiding it, there must be something about which he was ashamed, something he could not and would not discuss. And when she asked him, he denied and protested too much. So the long trail of her thinking ended in only one conclusion—a woman.

Muriel hated herself when she went to the detective agency and paid for a man to follow Rod when he went out for several nights during that week. But she told herself it was for his own good and the good of their marriage. And maybe it wasn't a woman and she was only imagining that Rod had in some subtle way changed. It wouldn't do any harm to find out. And she certainly couldn't follow him herself, even if she would.

But it *was* a woman, the report said. Andrea Tedesco. He always went straight to her apartment from their house. And remained for hours. She remembered the name and knew who it was. Miss Tedesco had been his secretary about a month while Miss Cadman, a perfectly safe little thing of nearly sixty, was in the hospital. But she had never had occasion to meet Miss Tedesco and now she had to see for herself.

So she went to the address with the detective one afternoon about the time Miss Tedesco should be getting home from work. And she sat in the detective's car and waited until the detective said, "There, that's the one coming up the street now, in the powder-blue dress."

Well, Muriel could see that the girl was young and attractive in a flashy sort of way. She would have sex appeal, and not much else. So Muriel felt worse and, at the same time, better. Because Miss Tedesco wouldn't last. She had a spark that set Rod on fire but the fire would go out if it was left alone and there would be nothing but the ashes of a cheap little affair. So Muriel had the detective put her in a cab, she went on home and said nothing about it.

It was Muriel's belief that Rod was already conscience-stricken and full of self-condemnation. The very worst thing she could do was to accuse him and when he denied it, show her proof with righteous anger. In that case, one of two things might happen. Caught in the act, embarrassed and contrite, Rod would despise himself. And every time he looked at Muriel, he would see her, not as his loving wife, but as a walking accusation, a reminder that he should loathe himself. And probably

38

loathe her more for making him feel the guilt. There might be a widening and permanent breach. Or, on the other hand, he could become so angry at her spying and discovering, he might be driven still deeper into the arms of Miss Andrea Tedesco.

No, the best thing was to say nothing and show nothing. The affair was a freak of circumstance. He had been thrown together with the wrong woman by an accident. He still loved her, Muriel. The affair would fall of its own weight since there was nothing but a cheap thrill to support it. Muriel would maintain silence.

But it didn't work out that way. Months later he was still seeing her. Only now, if he felt any guilt, she couldn't detect it. Habit had seemingly made him comfortable with the lie. And for the first time Muriel was beginning to doubt him and to feel her own insecurity.

Always inclined to be on the heavy side, Muriel now began to take on weight in quantity. There were little snacks between meals—and during was an occasion for stuffing. She read incessantly for distraction and it became impossible to turn a page without a box of candy at her elbow. And the corner drugstore made those marvelous fudge sundaes and banana splits. And a hamburger and French fries always seemed so good with a soda . . .

All the weight went to her hips and buttocks. And to her face, which took on a bloated look. It was awful! She had to do something! So she went on endless diets. They all lasted about three days.

The amazing thing was that Rod never mentioned her appearance. If *she* brought it up, he would say something like, "Well, I suppose you should go on a diet. But don't take it too seriously, dear." He seemed absolutely unconcerned. Well, of course it didn't matter to him. Perhaps it made him feel justified with that Tedesco woman. And if he didn't care, she didn't either.

But now something had to be done about Andrea Tedesco, after which she would worry about her weight. So Muriel insistently proposed this month in Malibu. She would get him away from that influence. And then in just the right way and at just the right time, she would have a talk with him. She would have to tell him in a very kind manner that she had "guessed" there was another woman and, was it true? Distance would give him perspective and, since he really did, since he certainly

39

must still love her, that would be the end of it.

Muriel looked down to where Star Osborne still stood with her hand on that good-looking Humphrey boy's shoulder, talking to her husband while the Erickson kid fussed with that gruesome fish and that nice Mr. Royce helped him. Or was Mr. Royce so nice after all?

Last night she had been at the window when that woman had gone up the steps to his apartment, looking half potted. It was quite a surprise because she had been so remote until then, ignoring everyone, especially the men. And Muriel had remarked about it later to Rod, emphasizing that the woman was *still* there after two hours and God knew *when* she would be out, if at all. And Rod said "So what? If she wants to get laid, that's her own god-damn business." But Rod wasn't kidding her. That was just his way of talking. If not shocked—nothing shocked him—he was at least surprised. Why wouldn't he be at such a complete turnabout?

So, after all, was Mr. Royce so very nice? Well, he wasn't married and you couldn't really blame *him*.

And now there she was ignoring Mr. Royce, her hand on Jay Humphrey's shoulder and talking to Rod. Oh God, thought Muriel. That's just the sort of thing we came down here to get away from. If Rod plays around right in front of me . . . Oh God, God! Wouldn't you know? Just when I thought everything was going so well.

nine

Bruce Erickson was behind the camera, ready to take the picture of Star and the shark. Jay stood next to him, watching her, a little possessive smile on his face which said now it was only a question of time. Erickson tried to keep the smile from irritating him, but even as he adjusted the camera, the smile was seared on his brain. Royce, after helping with the shark, had left, walking up the beach with Lindquist.

A nail had been driven into the wood trim of the building in order to suspend the shark which had been gaffed through the upper jaw. A heavy thong in the gaff handle was looped over the nail. The shark's tail just cleared the sand, the down-pull of weight on the jaw causing the mouth to gape widely with a predatory display of angry teeth. Star stood next to the shark, holding upright a rod and reel in one hand, harpoon in the other, drawing back her lips for the smile. In the viewfinder, Erickson was seeing his own special picture.

Beautiful, he thought. Beautiful! That hair falls so long and shiny . . . way it touches her shoulders . . . soft, like a caress. Want to smell it, smother in it. Like to kiss that mouth . . . soft . . . floating away . . . soft. Damn. Oh, damn. Waiting all the god-damn years for this one. Want this one. Got to have 'er. Got to!

"Well," she was saying, "don't just stand there, Bruce boy. Your wheels locked or something? Take the pretty picture."

"Sure," he said. "Sure, Star. Waiting for that big smile. Say cheese."

"Cheese—cake," said Jay, and the grin was there in his voice.

Erickson frowned.

"You can't smile with cake in your mouth," said Star.

"I wasn't thinking of your mouth," said Jay in that bold don't-give-a-damn way of his. "Not right then, anyway."

He got by with that crack because she was laughing, they were both laughing. God damn.

But while she was laughing, Erickson took the picture.

"C'mon, Jay," said Star. "Now one of you and me and sharky together. Just the three of us. Real cozy."

Looking pleased, Humphrey went over and got on the other side of the shark, then changed his mind and stood next to Star with his arm around her, one hand dangling down in front so that it nearly touched her breast.

She's embarrassed, thought Bruce. But look at her smiling. Pretends she doesn't notice. Wish he wouldn't do that. He should know better. He really should. Wonder if she'll ask me to stand with her for the next one?

He turned the roll and took the picture.

"Well, that's it," said Humphrey, taking her hand and walking her out from the building. "How about a swim?"

Erickson felt disappointed but was afraid to mention that he wanted his picture taken with her now. "We ought to get rid of the shark," he said. "And clean up the gear, put the motor away."

"We'll do it later," said Humphrey, stripping off the green coveralls underneath which he wore only his red bathing trunks. "Too damn hot now. Besides I want to wash off the stink of fish." He dropped the coveralls on the sand, took the rod and harpoon from Star and laid them on top. "You want to come along, Bruce? Do you good."

His voice was friendly and inclusive, but his eyes said, I'll hate your guts if you say yes.

"No thanks," said Bruce. "I'll get started with the gear and when you come back you can help me haul the shark up the beach and bury the damn thing. Stupid to bring that bloody mess home in the first place."

"C'mon! Go for a swim with us," said Humphrey, more insistent now that he was sure he got his point across.

"Some other time."

"See you then, Bruce."

Star gave Bruce a broad wink and raced after Humphrey to the water.

Bruce picked up the rod and the harpoon and carried them to the boat where it rested beside the building. He placed both inside and for a moment stood considering if he should get a rag and start wiping down the hull and mopping the slime off the deck. He didn't feel like it. The hell with it. Let Jay carry his own pack. He sank to the sand and leaned against the bow, absently watching Star and Jay treading water just a foot apart beyond the breakers.

The resentment was beginning to churn inside him. And because it was a new and unpleasant feeling and had no right to be there, he grew still more sullen. It was the first real gap in his affection for Jay and the gap was widening right while he sat there watching them together in the water. Probably their legs were touching beneath the surface, if he knew Jay Humphrey.

The whole thing was silly. It wasn't Humphrey's fault. And it certainly wasn't Star's. How could the poor girl know that from the first moment he set eyes on her, that first time when a few days ago she came cool and distant to the beach, he was lost. All tied up and tense inside. Gone. Gone, all right, but not mentioning it to Jay because he would take a ribbing, a lot of dirty stuff that would spoil the sweet bubbling inside him. Women

42

were mostly just shack-jobs to Jay. And that was all right. But Jay couldn't tell one from another.

No, it wasn't Jay's fault. Jay saw bait like that shark and went after it without thinking. And, after all, how could he know? And if he did, Bruce wondered, what then? Certainly it would make a difference. They had been friends a long time. A long, long time. Close. Very close.

He owed Jay a lot. A whole hell of a lot. Yes, he did. No getting away from it. Before Korea and Easy Company—not so god-damnned easy, either— with Jay in the same platoon, he was nothing, had nothing. He shoved gas into jalopies at a cut-rate service station. Cheap gas, a cheap job. And lived in a ten-dollar-a-week room in Glendale. Ate at Al's greasy spoon—punch your ticket for another batch of slop. The old culinary T. S. card. And had only one really good suit of clothes and a '36 Dodge. His father was dead. His mother, who used him but never had any use for him, worked in a laundromat and was remarried to a drunken bastard who didn't work at all.

That was his life. And to tell the truth the army came as a kind of relief. When Clint Sully, one of the guys he soldiered with, said, "Look at that sonofabitch eat. That Bruce, he found a home when he came to the god-damn army," Sully didn't know he wasn't exactly kidding. There was a certain feeling in the army. You hated it—but so did everyone else in his right mind. And it was another kind of loneliness. All lonely together.

He was even in the same squad with Jay, was second in command to him, and they just naturally got together. Nothing big. Just sharing the same slice of hell. And then it got deeper. You couldn't exactly say when. Maybe when Hager fell dead just after he pulled the pin and dropped the grenade right by Jay's foot. And Bruce leaped and made a lightning grab for it, hurling it just in time. Maybe the day they were careless with fatigue and disgust, moving forward almost three abreast against all good sense and training, with Sal Gribaldi in the center. The hidden machine gun should have knocked them all down like three pins in a row. Yet it didn't. It cut Sal almost in half, but they were not even nicked, he and Jay, lying prone in their own fear-sweat, but nevertheless turning at the same time to look at each other and smile in a grim sort of way. Maybe at that moment. Who could tell when it began? But anyhow, they had a thing going together and it didn't

43

quit with the truce but lasted after their discharge.

The boat works was a father-and-son deal at the time and Humphrey had given him a small job, moving him from department to department, shifting him so he would learn the business. Humphrey had never made him feel like an employee but more like it was Humphrey and Son—and friend. Bruce was in on all the big decisions and his advice was sought. He had never felt so important, so needed and so proud in his whole life.

Then, when Jay's father fell off the ladder and died in that crazy accident, Jay had made him a partner. Not a full partner. But he had given him twenty per cent of the net business above his salary and had *called* him a partner. It gave him a very warm, a very peculiar feeling, like nothing he had ever experienced.

Would he ever forget the way he first heard that he was to be a partner, over at Wenzel Marine, one of their retail outlets? Humphrey had placed an arm around his shoulder affectionately as they stood in Mr. Wenzel's office and had announced in a ceremonious voice, "Mr. Wenzel, I'd like to have you meet my new partner, Bruce Erickson."

He just stood there dumbly, looking at Jay and then at Mr. Wenzel, rising behind the desk with outstretched hand. For the longest moment he couldn't say anything, fighting a convulsive urge to cry, Mr. Wenzel's hand suspended in the air as though it were detached and separate and might fall unheeded with a horror of embarrassment at any second.

Outside on the street he had caught Jay by the arm and stopped him in stride, looking up into his face. What he wanted to say was, I love you, you sonofabitch. I love you. But all he could bring out was, "Thanks, Jay. Gee, thanks a hell of a lot."

But oh, how he worked after that. How he studied those boats to improve their design. How he went out with his big faith in their beauty and utility and sold them until they couldn't keep up with the demand. You would have thought he had the eighty per cent cut out of that pie and Jay the twenty instead of the other way around.

And now he had a big convertible, new one every year, a nice little two-bedroom house with Jay, a closet full of sport jackets and suits, and a bank balance in five

44

figures. And he owed all that to Jay, yes he did.

Though now the thought came to him that, while it was true Jay took him in and gave him a start, Jay was no dumb-bell or philanthropist. Jay knew he was a worker, a pusher. And smart. He had ideas and he could sell. Jay didn't give him that twenty per cent for nothing. No sir! He had earned it. He had really earned and was entitled to a full partnership.

Jay and Star were coming in out of the surf now, stumbling and laughing and shoving each other playfully. Jay acted like he had known her a year, like he already owned her.

Jay had always owned some part, a big part, of everything he touched—both people and things. Some people were the owners, the havers. The others were the have-nots, the serfs who took what was left when the master's table was cleared. All his life Bruce had been one of the have-nots, not even a has-been, but a never-was. He had owned nothing. But now he owned that twenty per cent. It wasn't much, but he did have that. What he didn't have and wanted most now was a woman. His woman.

Watching the long swing of Humphrey's legs going away down the beach, hard muscle of shoulder and bicep touching against the soft flesh of Star beside him, Bruce wished he didn't owe so much. It was a bad thing to be in debt to someone, even your best friend. Maybe especially your best friend. A very bad thing. Because then if you saw something you wanted which he already had his careless hands on, wanted more than the twenty per cent and the car and the clothes and the money in the bank, you couldn't do anything about it. Not a god-damn thing. You could just sit there and watch it slowly being taken. And maybe soiled in the taking, the way an animal would soil some priceless rug—with the same unthinking indifference—a rug was a rug.

Yes, it was a very bad thing, this needing and this owing at the same time. And maybe it was almost as bad that Jay was beginning to look different to him in some sad-subtle way. Some of the shine had gone out of his face and the graceful swing of his limbs moving away was not graceful at all but full of ugly power. And the broad back was a wall—a wall of aggression.

45

"We should have brought a robe," said Jay Humphrey beside her. "Lousy sand sticks like ground glass."

"I didn't know we were going to make this a picnic," said Star. "I would have packed a lunch. God! I'm exhausted. Those big waves tossed me around like a doll. And my hair is a mess!" She sighed. Her voice took on a drowsy quality. "It feels so good to lie down. So good."

They lay in a small gully of sand, the slopes of which barely concealed them from view. Behind them was an empty lot overgrown with tall grass. In the distance they could hear the whine and swish of traffic along 101. The beach immediately surrounding them was deserted.

Humphrey sank down, adjusting himself so that his leg appeared to come into accidental contact with hers. Digging his elbow into the sand, he supported the weight of his head in the palm of his hand and looked down upon her, studying her body while he had the chance, while her eyes were closed.

Christ Almighty, what a hunk of stuff! Maybe she isn't exactly the most beautiful girl I've ever seen, her features aren't altogether perfect and she's a little hefty in spots, but she sure is the sexiest. Man, you could eat that all up like peaches and cream and come back for seconds. Wonder if she's been had? Jerk! What you mean is, how many times? Who cares, brother? Who cares! Just let me have mine. Just give me one little room and a bed, stack it with this one and plenty of food and you wouldn't see me for three days. I wouldn't come out if someone pushed a button and the god-damn third world war was on. Man!

"You going to sleep on me?" he murmured.

"Unh-uh."

"You sure are a chameleon."

"What does that mean?" Her eyes remained closed, her voice had a fuzzy-soft remoteness.

"Just about what it says. A chameleon will have one of those cool colors—like green—next thing you know

46

it slithers into a new environment and it turns one of those hot colors, like, say, a kind of dusty red-brown. Hot, you know. But sometimes a chameleon will stand still in the same environment, not move an inch, and yet it will change colors anyway. And you ask yourself, what made it do that? You can't figure it out—cool one minute, hot the next."

"Maybe the little thing was embarrassed at something and just flushed red."

"Oh, no, don't give me that dodge. If I looked a chameleon right in the eye and asked it an honest question, I'd expect an honest answer."

"My eyes are closed."

"Hah."

"But I read once that a chameleon has moods and these moods affect its color."

"Well, that may be true and I'd accept it from an honest chameleon. But, baby, you were in that freezer, locked right in. And then something happened and the door opened and you came right out into the sunshine. So who or what opened the door?"

"Is it so important?"

"Not especially. Just curious."

"I like your friend Bruce. A very sweet guy."

"Now you change the subject. Sure, he's a good kid. The best."

"Why do you call him a kid? Are you so much older? You don't look it."

"About two years older. But I do think of him as a kid, like a younger brother, I guess. That's because I look out for him. He always needed someone to do that, though he wouldn't admit it. And I took the job."

"He looks husky enough to look out for himself."

"Husky, smushky, you don't get the point. It takes more than muscle to look out for yourself in this goddamn world. You've got to be hard where it counts—inside. You've got to keep shoving back or the phonies will swarm all over you and pick your bones. You've got to look into their minds and see the crumby motives hiding behind their fat smiling faces."

He looked down at her and her eyes were now open, alert with interest and curiosity. "The trouble with Bruce," he continued, "is that he's soft. Basically, he's soft. He never had anything, he was practically a bum when I

47

gave him his first decent job. He was kicked around at home and everywhere else, he went through a god-damn bloody war, and still he can't tell a snake from a rabbit. He thinks people are great—the greatest. Even me." He chuckled. "And he should know me better than anyone."

She said nothing. She lay on her back with her head pillowed on hands folded behind her head. Her eyes drooped and closed again. Even in repose there was a trace of sneering impatience about her abundant mouth, an angry set to her soft-hard chin. Her cheeks pouted, her whole face was a demand. Her body had a lithe-cat indolence—stretched and harmless-seeming—while inside the coiled animal thing, restless and tense, still paced and paced.

Humphrey watched the wild grass bowing with every little gust of wind. Distant sounds faded and the hush was immediate, private. Wind and sea murmured in a sun-warm vacuum. He felt separate in an isolated moment of peace. But the peace did not include Star Osborne. Sifting sand through his fingers he looked out across the ruffle of ocean to the horizon.

Of course the kid was goofy about this bitch with her hungry body. He had known that almost from the beginning, pretending he hadn't the least idea. It wasn't a matter of competition or anything childish like that. Hell, he didn't give a damn. The world was full of babes, though admittedly this one might be the juiciest piece of all. But that had nothing to do with it, really. Bruce had the look. In his eyes you could see his knees crumbling right down to the ground, hands upraised to the goddess, the worship written all over his puss as he knelt below the pedestal. He knew that look. Once in a while it had been there for him—the worship without the passion, a naked idolizing that was a little uncomfortable and embarrassing, though not unwanted. Hell, why shouldn't the kid idolize him a little? He was father-mother-brother-sister—the works—the whole family to him. He had given him practically everything he ever had worth the god-damn powder to blow it up.

But this was different, this jazz with the Osborne bitch. Like he said, Bruce didn't know a snake from a rabbit. It was all right to kneel down before a rabbit and play cuddles for a while. It wouldn't do you any good but it wouldn't do you any harm either. But when you kneel

48

down before a cobra, female or not, it is going to give you a nice cozy bite right between the eyes. And that love-poison was going to seep into your system and go right down to your soul or wherever you lived, and poison it. And then, brother, if you were Bruce Erickson, you'd be a dead duck. But if you were Jay Humphrey, you had a tough hide and maybe no damn soul at all and you were immune. There wasn't a woman he'd met yet who could touch him all the way down to where he lived. And when it did happen it wouldn't be one like this. No, ma'am. He could see right into this one—see the whole twisted works spinning away like crazy—the spring too tight, the wheels not meshing and out of control.

She would try to ruin every poor bastard she touched and she would keep touching and moving on to the next one until that whole mess inside ran down or exploded. And it wasn't going to happen to a nice kid like Bruce. Not if he could help it. He knew what was good for Bruce. He always had known exactly what was good for Bruce. Hadn't he proved that? And now he was just protecting him from the poison fangs. Just protecting him, that's all.

So the best way to handle it was not to tell him—you couldn't tell him about a thing like this—but to show him. He would play dumb and while he was playing dumb he would show Bruce exactly what made this one tick. He would open her up for inspection. And when Bruce saw what was there, he would run fast. Or, at least, he would grow up a bit. Yeah, he might just grow up. Do him a lot of good.

The thought made him feel strong and protective and righteous all at once. For the kid's own good.

Quietly he swung part way over her, hoisting himself just above her face. His shadow nudged her awareness and she opened her eyes slowly. The face was closed from emotion—cold. But the eyes coming to his face already focused and alert, said something of cunning knowledge about him, so secret and evil he almost shuddered.

"I've been expecting you," she said. "Where have you been?"

"Not far, baby, not far. If you were a snake, you would have bitten me." He let go and fell across her. Her mouth opened and swallowed his lips. Her tongue wound over his in a sinuous entwining. Ecstasy throbbed and crashed

49

inside him with a thundering urgency. Her hands came from behind her head, hair spilling into sand. One hand held him fast about the neck, the other explored, winding down his side.

He tore his lips from hers, growled hoarsely into the red gape of her mouth, "That's it, baby. That's it. You know where you're going and so do I."

"No," she said. "Not here. We'd swallow each other up and a whole crowd could be watching and we wouldn't even notice. Besides, for this you need time. Lots and lots of time, darling. You come down to my apartment tonight. And when you leave you'll wonder where you've been and what you've been doing all these years. I'll own you then. But you won't care."

She began to laugh. It was an odd, broken and mirthless chuckling.

"You'll never own me, baby," he said. "No one will ever own me. But we'll have a time. We'll have a time you won't forget. Because I know you, baby. I dig you way down inside where you're hiding. Some little part of me is just like that great big part of you. In that way we're two of a kind, baby. I feel it but I can't explain it to myself. So I'm going to dredge you out and have a look at you. But, oh man, oh woman, we'll have a time!"

She had become quiet and was peering at him with a searching amusement. "Yes, we'll have a time, darling," she said. Then she began that mirthless laugh again—on and on.

eleven

"She's a queer one, all right," said Rod Lindquist to Royce. "Before you came she was quite different, you know. A regular recluse. Hardly spoke to the women and wouldn't bother with the men at all." He turned to look at Royce, keeping his face casual so that he wouldn't be thought too nosy. "What is this hypnotic power that you have, Royce? Even the frigid ones come under the spell."

"I don't think she ever was frigid," said Royce. "Not in her whole life. Remote or angry, maybe. Not frigid.

50

But if she really did change, and she certainly seemed to, I didn't get the impression it had anything to do with me. She was just as disdainful of me as anyone—at first."

They had been walking along the beach. Lindquist was bored with the fish episode and had invited Royce to hike with him to a spot the other side of the Malibu Pier. Here there must have been a shoal of sorts because the waves broke far out, providing a long fast run for the surfboarders. They rode the great down-spill of the waves recklessly, often standing straight and proud and in perfect balance, hurtling all the way in to shore. It looked dangerous; it was a rather thrilling sight and Lindquist wanted to watch.

Muriel had said she didn't care to join them—she had a roast to stick in the oven—and then she was going shopping at the grocers. Since they were already overstocked with supplies, this probably meant she was headed for the Malibu Inn and a fudge sundae. So he and Royce had gone off alone to see the surf-riders, chatting about nothing of particular importance. Now they were trudging slowly back and inevitably the subject of Star Osborne had sneaked into the conversation.

"So she was disdainful of you, too," said Lindquist. "But only at first?"

"That's right," said Royce. "Only at first." His voice sounded just a little bit guarded.

"I didn't mean to pry," said Lindquist quickly. "Just curious like anyone else. Nothing personal there, I hope."

"Oh, hell no," said Royce. "Far from it."

"Good. Because I think she's something of a troublemaker, don't you?"

"If she doesn't make trouble it won't be because she isn't trying."

"The women obviously don't like her," said Lindquist. "And the men like her too much. That could make for a situation. I wish we could get her the hell out of here."

Royce kicked a mound of sand with his toe. "Got any ideas?"

"Not at the moment," said Lindquist. "She's not exactly what you call a movable object. She looks like she could resist a cyclone on a bicycle."

"The cyclone's inside of her," said Royce. "I can't figure her out. But I'll tell you this. She's got more than hot pants. She's got a purpose. It's a very insidious thing."

"Muriel said she looked boozed up last night."

"She was."

"Oh? How do you know?"

Royce seemed to hesitate. "She came to my apartment."

"What did she want?"

"Said she was bored and wanted to talk."

"Talk? Huh!"

Royce was silent.

"I know what you mean," said Lindquist. "It isn't good to gossip about a woman that way. Even if she acts like a whore."

Royce looked out to sea, pursing his lips. There was a hard clarity and strength in his profile, a classic refinement. Lindquist decided he was a pretty decent guy. "Well, I don't know," said Royce. "I was never very good at the sex post-mortem stuff. Even in bull sessions. On the one hand you're bragging because you caught the brass ring in the sex merry-go-round, and on the other you're accusing the ring for allowing itself to be caught. Even the tramps, so-called, are entitled to a little privacy. Everyone bows to their own god of indulgence, even if it's just being a self-righteous bastard."

"I guess that'll hold me," said Lindquist. "Anyway, I was more interested in what she had to say about herself. She seems a mystery. Did she mention where she comes from, why she's here, anything like that?"

"Says she's from Cleveland, was married to a rich guy who died and left her a pile. Came here for a vacation. Other than that, she might as well have dropped from the sky for all I got out of her."

"I wish she'd dropped somewhere else."

"You don't like her, I take it."

"No, I don't like her. But I'll admit she's tempting. And my God, I can't afford to be tempted. Not that she shows any interest—in me."

"When I get married," said Royce picking up a shell, scaling it into the water, "she'll be enough woman so I won't be tempted very often."

Royce began a story about a producer he knew who was married to one of the most beautiful girls Royce had ever seen. But played around on the side with a babe who was almost as homely as his wife was beautiful. Royce was discussing the psychological aspect, but Lindquist wasn't listening. He was hearing again what Royce had said just the moment before, "When I get married, she'll be enough woman so I won't be tempted very often."

Well, it didn't happen because Muriel wasn't enough woman. Muriel had always been plenty of woman for him at bed level or any other level. In truth, he hadn't married like some men, just because they were bed-happy. There was a time when he had even wondered fleetingly if he wasn't a bit on the sub-normal side in the sex department. He had never been much of a run-around before he was married, preferring to stick with one girl until the relationship ran out of whatever fuel was propelling it and just died from lack of nourishment. Then he would pass on to someone else and the cycle would begin again.

Most women were terrible bores after you scratched the first bright coat of veneer off their conversation. As for that sex drool, he always had the feeling that women just endured it as the price they had to pay for any kind of continuity in male companionship. It was all an act and he could sense a yawn behind every little fake sigh and whimper of passion. His reaction to this form of pretense was to want to laugh right out loud. Not a big hearty laugh, but something in an echo chamber—hollow and bitter—at the funny-sad tricks life played on you. And just as soon as he couldn't take the other half, the partner in the Big Game, seriously, he lost interest. Why bother with a charade in which you're the only one who's trying?

"So of course it seemed obvious to me," Royce was saying, "that beautiful or not, his wife was just an ornament and this homely one, this mistress, if you want to call her that, was giving him whatever it really was he had to have to fill the void."

Lindquist nodded absently. "I suppose you're right. Good point."

Muriel was quite different from the others, though. She didn't have an insincere bone in her body. She was a big soft puppy, lovable and insecure as all puppies, deep but surface-shy, crying for love. And out of her big needing she gave all of herself—in bed, out of bed, every waking hour. And Lindquist had found that this was the prize, that only in such needing was there any real giving.

And Muriel had astonished him at her wisdom and

53

understanding. It had been there all the time. But she had, with her soft-stepping, timid approach to life, been lacking in the confidence of expression which he had slowly built in her. Not that she ever seemed to change for other people—only for him—in their private hours.

They never knew the ugly silences of mutual boredom. They stimulated each other, never ran out of topics. It was like a contest, the exchange of ideas. The sensual was there, too, but at rest—not strident, not disturbingly insistent. And anyway, Lindquist had thought, what the hell, life is mostly vertical, not horizontal. And the best part of the union is companionable and conversational, not physical.

Of course, they had their arguments. Christ, yes! Who didn't? But they were quick flare-ups that burned themselves out in an hour or two, not smoldering resentments. And altogether he loved Muriel with such a violent tenderness he concealed it with a rough, an almost crude exterior.

"You would think," said Royce, "that if he liked this other cookie—the homely one—he would divorce the glamor girl. But no, nothing of the kind. So naturally you have to conclude that . . ."

It was strange how fooled you were about yourself. You thought you had it all figured out—the loving wife, the dear little girl, the fine house, the big business, the plentiful income—no problems, no needs, everywhere satisfied. As far as you could see in any direction it was all good. But what you hadn't understood, hadn't even guessed, was that sometimes you didn't know all that you desired in the secret convolutions of your being until it walked in on its handsome stockinged legs and offered itself.

Andrea Tedesco. God-damn that Cadman woman, such a nice old lady, for ever getting sick and going to the hospital. What was it, gall stones? He couldn't even remember now. But on the day Miss Cadman phoned in sick, they sent Andrea up from the typing pool. She was young and pretty and she had raven-black hair and wide insolent eyes and a figure that turned your gaze everyway but loose. She came in with her brisk proud manner to take dictation, sitting straight but crossing and uncrossing her long legs while suggesting, rather impertinently but rightly, little changes in phrasing. "Don't you think, Mr. Lindquist, it might be more tactful to say," or "I don't think that's quite clear, sir. You might put it this way."

She irritated him, but she was almost always right and when she saw he was annoyed, that she had spoken out of turn, she had a way of bending her head down humbly, biting her lip, her eyes raised up at him in a teasing—oh, I was naughty, wasn't I?—attitude. It was charming, charming!

She was the soul of neatness and terribly efficient. She had things done before they entered his mind! Slowly she wormed her way into his confidence—was really trying to worm her way into his office for keeps—and subtlely caused him to lose nearly everything of formality. In three days' time, he was calling her Andrea and in a week she was calling him Rod, darling—and doing this over Martinis in her apartment.

"But actually," Royce droned on, "he's a good guy. Just mixed up. Aren't we all? Anyhow, the climax of the whole thing came when . . ."

Of course Lindquist knew that she was a climber and thought she could handle something big in the company if he gave her the chance. But he was still flattered. He had never considered himself a great lover or anything like that. But she made him feel he was. And for the first time in his life, he went almost crazy with basic, unadulterated, but adulterous physical needing.

Instead of giving her a raise and the big job she sought, he had her resign the day after Cadman came back and she returned to the pool. Then he got her a new apartment—an elegant layout furnished to his taste—a new car, unlimited clothes and three times her salary in spending money. It was insane! But irresistible.

Guilt took over immediately. He could hardly look Muriel in the eye. He drove himself to please her, loved her more than ever—perhaps in sympathy—and couldn't, absolutely couldn't, stay removed from Andrea more than a couple days, though she had nothing which he really wanted—but her body.

Muriel, poor Muriel. She was so sensitive. She felt something was going on, that she had lost some part of him, and began to lapse into her old insecurity. Was that why she ate all the time? Christ! Oh, God-damn! So that when she said she had to have a change—why didn't they call Macklin and reserve a place at the Tides where they had vacationed once before?—he couldn't refuse her. And thought maybe in the interval he would find strength to tell Andrea it was over.

"Because after you've been around a while," said Royce, "you find out that most beautiful women are lousy lovers. They're all takers. Spoiled rotten. They have nothing to give. In bed they're just manikins. Manikins, that's all."

"I suppose that's true," said Lindquist. "But I don't have much experience with beautiful women."

With Lindquist dreaming and Royce oblivious in his story, they had gone past the Pacific Tides and had come now to a section of deserted beach where there was an open field of wild grass. Royce pulled up abruptly and held him back with an extended arm.

"What's the matter?" said Lindquist.

Royce didn't answer but gave a little nod of his head toward the foreground. And now Lindquist could see that they were almost on top of a narrow depression in the sand. Then he heard the giggling and could just make out the red bathing trunks and a small patch of gold blending together.

"I'll be god-damned!" he muttered. "Well for Christ sake! C'mon, Royce, let's go back."

twelve

That same night at five minutes after ten o'clock by Royce's watch, the entire group—all except Star Osborne—were still seated on the patio drinking beer and making small-talk. Royce noticed the time because this was when Humphrey got up to leave.

It was not so much a social gathering as one of expediency. Even in the summer, and especially at the beach, the California nights were usually cool. You seldom slept without at least one blanket. But now the wind had died, the air had not given up the heat of the day and the torpid atmosphere stifled breathing and clung to the body like a hot towel in a steam bath. Everyone but Star Osborne had come outdoors to escape.

The conversation, Royce had noticed, held a tense and

56

rather forced conviviality. There were long pauses and the talk had the disjointed, groping flavor of people who give the largest attention to the area of their private thoughts.

If there was an exception, it was Laura Bishop. She sat next to Humphrey and pushed her words at the circle with staccato bursts of enthusiasm which died from lack of response. It seemed clear to Royce that while she spoke to the group at large, she was trying pathetically to impress Humphrey, who merely nodded, yawned and shifted in his chair as he glanced more and more often in the direction of Star Osborne's apartment.

Normally conservative in her dress, tonight Laura had decked herself in a strapless pink and black frock which for the first time revealed that she had a damn good figure when she wasn't hiding it. She had also taken her hair down and given herself gentle waves at the forehead. Falling darkly around her face, the sweep of it gave her features a soft appeal. Her appearance had lost the impression of austerity. To Royce, she seemed now a very pretty girl. But if this had the least impression on Humphrey, it wasn't apparent. For at five minutes after ten he glanced again toward the Osborne apartment, said, "Guess I'll go find out what's happened to Star. She must be smothering."

In the prominent hush that followed, he got up and went to her door. In a moment the door opened and he disappeared inside. Looks were passed around and then slowly the conversation resumed. At this point Royce had a little side exchange with Laura. For all her distractions, she seemed a deep and interesting person. Royce found himself liking her immensely.

At midnight when the gathering broke up, Humphrey had still not returned. Watching their faces, it seemed to Royce that this was of most concern to Laura Bishop and Bruce Erickson. Laura looked pinched and nervous, Bruce dark and sullen. Royce could already sense the coming of trouble.

But on the following day Star Osborne showed neither interest nor animosity for Humphrey. She simply ignored him. Just before noon, Royce saw her drive off somewhere with Bruce Erickson. They didn't return until after nightfall. Everyone knew that Erickson remained most of the next two nights in her apartment.

57

By this time the pattern was clear to Royce. He knew Rod Lindquist would be next. And he was right—up to a point. For though she tried at every opportunity to at least get Lindquist into private conversation, he remained aloof. Royce was certain this was not a matter of choice, but rather self-protection. For Muriel was never far away. And deep in her placid face, her eyes were moving and watchful.

What Humphrey felt, if anything, he masked. It was as if he gave a mental shrug. He promptly returned to Laura Bishop and they were together constantly.

Another truth now became evident to Royce. There had been no peculiar or hidden meaning in Star's anger toward him on the day following his single night with her. She simply expected that he would continue to be available to her—the ever faithful and love-hungry slave. In that last meeting on the beach, she was merely testing the degree of his enchantment in proposing the picnic. Then when she found he wasn't ready to grab his things and run, she displayed the temper and driving will of a woman who had to possess, who had seldom if ever been scorned. But with so many other conquests behind her, she must now have forgotten him.

Four nights later, Bruce Erickson was still the Queen's consort and devoted lover, Laura was restored to the arms of Humphrey, and Muriel and Rod Lindquist apparently enjoyed whatever bond had held them from the beginning.

Then came the night of the party held by Star Osborne in her apartment. All were invited and all came. Yet it was a strange party in that the guests consented with a certain foreboding, not really wanting to attend, but nevertheless unable to resist an event in which there was a certain bent curiosity. For where there was Star Osborne, there was excitement and trouble. And this was her first appearance with her entire retinue.

Long afterward Royce observed that all might have gone reasonably well. But there was too much hate. And too much love. And far too much alcohol. And these were not ingredients for anything but disaster.

58

PART TWO

one

"C'mon, c'mon!" said Bruce Erickson, pulling on the trousers to his tan tropical. "You gonna sit there and guzzle? It's twenty-five of. Party's at nine."

Humphrey, naked to the waist, sat slumped in a chair, sipping a highball morosely. "Don't know if I'll bother with the god-damn party," he muttered.

"Why not? Why not!" Erickson was shining his shoes with a torn handkerchief. "What about Laura? She's expecting you to take her."

"Laura, Laura, virgin-aura." He chuckled. "Nice kid, but no future. Not for me, buddy. Not for me." He sounded a little thick. He had been drinking steadily for the last hour and for no reason apparent to Erickson.

"Well, Star's expecting you, too, you know."

"Star, Star—har, har."

"Can it."

"Why should I go? She's nothing to me. And that's what she should be to you, too, kiddo. Nothing."

"Can it, will you?"

"No, god-damn it! I mean it. She's gonna give you a pain where you don't need it. She's no good. Leave 'er alone."

Erickson's hand, busy shining the shoe, paused in mid-stroke. He could feel the anger knotting inside him. "I wish you'd shut up, Jay," he said quietly. "Just shut up,

59

will you? You've been at it ever since she came over to me. Who are you to say she's good or bad? A few days ago, you thought she was the greatest."

"The greatest—"

"The greatest what? Go ahead, say it."

"The greatest lay in Malibu Beach—or any other beach."

Erickson dropped the handkerchief carefully in the waste basket, started across the room with clenched fists, turned abruptly at the center and went to a window, looking out, hands on hips. "I don't like that kind of talk, Jay," he said more quietly than ever, though at that moment he could have driven his fist through the pane in front of him. "Especially since it's not true. Star likes to pretend she's wild and easy, but it's only her way of having a little fun. She told me. And I believe her."

Lying next to her in the dark, naked, the cigarettes glowing, ocean boiling gently outside the open window, he had said, "Honey, I don't want you to think it's important. Actually it doesn't matter at all. But Jay is my best friend and I have to look the bastard in the eye and know the score. So—was there anything between you two —you know, like this?"

She giggled, a soft intimate sound in the darkness. "Do you think if there was I'd tell you, sweetie?"

"Sure you would, honey. If I asked you. And I'm asking."

"Well, I kissed him a few times."

"But that's all?"

"That's all. You think I don't know his type? I mean, he's your friend and I wouldn't say anything against him. He's not a bad guy. Just for kicks. But not for anything serious. Why do you think I dropped him cold? Women are nothing to him. Play toys."

"You don't hurt my feelings. I know about Jay. He doesn't mean any real harm. But I'm glad you didn't mess with him. Because I love you, honey. My God, my God, how I love you. Oh, Jesus, don't play with me the way he does with the babes he chases. It would kill me. You see, I never had anyone to love. In my whole life I never had anyone to love like this."

"Listen, lamb, you don't have to worry. I'm a born

flirt. I like to tease. But when anyone wants me to back it up, I run for the hills. You're such a sweet kid to care. I think you're the first one who ever did care, way down deep inside. It gives me a very odd feeling. I can't explain it."

She sounded so sincere, almost as if she were going to cry. "A very odd feeling?" he said. "Love?"

"Love, baby. Yes, love. That's it. A kind of love."

And now Jay Humphrey was saying, "Believe her? Huh! Don't believe anything she says. I don't. I never did. That's why I can get along with her and you can't without losing your soul. A guy could be in bed with her and she'd swear she's as pure as snow. That's how I believe her."

Erickson came around quickly. The bones in his hands ached. He felt the spasm of a cheek muscle. His arm came up and he aimed a finger at Jay, like a gun. "Listen, god-damn it!" he shouted. "That's it. That's enough! How many years, and did we ever have a fight? A real fight? You trying to start one now? Because I'll break you in half and you can shove the partnership!" His voice was crumbling. He could feel himself on the edge. There were tears just behind the jam of anger.

"All right," said Humphrey placatingly. "All right, forget it. I don't mean to needle, except to wake you up. You're asleep in that crazy pink and white world. And it's all going to fall in on you, collapse right on your head. Then you'll say, 'Why didn't you tell me, why didn't you tell me?' Well, kid, I've told you. And I could tell you a lot more. And what would it get me for my trouble but your big love-sick fist?"

"Okay," said Erickson with some feeling of relief. "Just keep it to yourself. I don't want to listen."

"Good boy!" said Humphrey. "Don't listen. Good boy. But I tell you she's using you. I don't know why. She uses everyone for some weird purpose of hers. And since you won't listen, I'm gonna have to *show* you. Maybe you'll believe what you see."

"Show me what?" said Erickson, beginning to feel uneasy.

"I'm gonna take the lid off for you, kid," said Humphrey. "I'm gonna let you have a peek into the sewer."

61

Erickson didn't have an answer. There was a certain honesty and conviction in Humphrey's tone that frightened him.

Humphrey set down his drink with a bang, stood and made for the bedroom.

"Now what?" said Erickson.

"Think I'll go to that party after all," said Humphrey over his shoulder. "Wouldn't miss it!"

"I'm just about ready," said Muriel, smoothing her skirt before the mirror, turning this way and that. "Do you like this thing? I don't know. I really don't. When I bought it—what was it?—a year ago?—when I bought it, I thought it was lovely. Just lovely. And now . . . I guess it's me, not the dress. But maybe I ought to change into something else. What do you think, Rod?"

Lindquist bent his head to the side and pretended to make a thoughtful study. It was a shantung suit, a very fine silk which he remembered had cost two hundred and a quarter. It was blue-gray with large white polka dots. At the time Muriel bought it, she was probably fifteen pounds thinner and the suit had seemed quite smart on her. But now it was too tight and anyway Muriel had too much weight to look good in a suit. It emphasized the spread of her hips. And the polka dots added somehow to her girth. No, the suit was a bad choice. On the other hand, he couldn't think of another outfit which would be much of an improvement. Lately, he thought sadly, Muriel had a slightly middle-aged appearance in everything she wore.

"It's a beautiful suit, dear," he said. "Very smart. It was always one of my favorites and you haven't worn it for a long time. I don't think you should change it."

"Maybe it's my hair," said Muriel, making furious little stabs at it. "Should be long. Don't know why I ever cut it. Just a silly whim, I guess. It's better to leave your hair long because every six months or so it's back in style again. You ready?"

"I'm ready."

"Honestly, darling, is there any reason at all why we should go to this thing? Everyone there will be single. We have nothing in common. Absolutely nothing. And I don't like that woman. She's an oversexed little tramp. I don't condemn her for that part. She has a right to her own life. But she's vicious, just vicious! She's playing

62

everyone against each other. Why? It's cruel. And it's bound to make trouble. Someone like that Erickson boy is going to take her seriously. And then, look out! Really, dear, what do those men see in her?"

Lindquist smiled. "Well now, that's a hard question to answer a woman. You would need a new set of equipment to appreciate her."

Muriel turned from the mirror to look at him, frowning. "Then you do appreciate her? I mean, you personally."

"Now, Muriel, this could get involved." He was still attempting to smile good humoredly as he looked at his watch. "And it's five of nine. We should be going."

"These days it's almost indecent to be on time. Besides, I really want to know."

"Want to know what?"

"Rod, for heaven's sake!"

"Well, yes. I think she has her own special kind of attraction—for someone."

"Someone?"

"Oh, my God! All right. Yes. There was a time when I might have found her quite a dish. Now, shall we go?" His temples throbbed. He felt a terrible irritation mounting in him tonight. Muriel must have seen him getting the come-on which he had resisted so beautifully up till now. But in spite of this, Muriel wasn't satisfied. She was digging at him in a strident manner that was completely unlike her. And while he sympathized with her, he was becoming angry. There were other pressures and worries knifing him. He wished he had never come on this trip. Andrea, Andrea, Andrea . . .

"Is it because she has such a nice figure, Rod? Is that it? Is that all you men ever care about? What about love and companionship and understanding that it takes years to build? I suppose to a man, all of that isn't worth one cheap thrill."

"Christ. Oh, Christ! No, there's nothing in the world like a good cheap thrill. Especially if it's cheap."

Muriel had walked over to the bureau and with her index finger was poking in a box of candy. After a moment's hesitation, she selected one and popped it into her mouth. She chewed on it slowly and, because her face had taken on an unaccustomed sullenness, the pout of her cheek where she held the nugget seemed to Lindquist lopsided and ugly. He was suddenly out of sympathy, loathing her indulgence. For a moment he almost wished he was rid of her. The thought shocked him and he erased it instantly.

"Well, if you want a cheap thrill, tonight's your chance." Muriel's voice came muffled around the hard chew of candy, moistly accusatory. "She's down there waiting. And you're next on the list."

"Muriel," said Lindquist sternly. "I want you to stop this. I don't know why, but you're feeling awfully god-damned sorry for yourself. It's a little sickening, don't you think?"

Muriel's mouth stopped chewing suddenly. "Is it be-cause—because I'm fat? Is that why other women have suddenly become attractive to you?"

Lindquist felt the swift return of all the old tenderness. Wasn't it really his fault? "Aw now, sweetheart, you know that isn't true," he said. "You may be a little plump, but you've never been fat." He went toward her with out-stretched arms. "I never could stand a skinny woman." He put his arms around her.

She twisted away from him. "I wish just once," she said, her voice rising, "that you wouldn't deny it. I wish you would care just enough about me to have the decency and honesty to admit I'm *just plain fat!*" She swallowed the last of her candy and went immediately to the box, plucked another and began the chewing all over again, her face more sullen than ever.

Lindquist could feel the heat rising and burning his face. "All right, god-damn it! You're fat. Just plain fat. You're getting to be a regular slob. You look eight months and twenty-nine days pregnant! Satisfied?"

The moment he had said it, he was sorry. But it was a little late. Muriel's mouth gave one last reflex chew on the candy and stopped. Her face began to crumple, flesh folding in upon itself, forming gullies of agony. She seemed to be squeezing the tears from her eyes one at a time. As soon as one scurried down her face and into her tor-tured mouth, another took its place. She was trying to make sounds but none would come. Then she didn't know what to do with the candy—that now distasteful lump in her mouth—so she kept shifting it about, finally bring-ing the soggy mass to rest under her tongue as she began to sob.

Lindquist had never seen a more pitiful, a more lost and lonely human being. At that moment he was more wretched than he had ever been in his life. The thought of all they had been to each other welled inside him. He crossed to her and put his arm around her, pulled her gently to him. "There, there, sweetheart, I didn't mean it. Not a word. I lost my temper. We all say things we don't mean to the ones we love most. And I do love you, Muriel dear. Don't feel empty, little girl. You always, always, have me. And this whole thing is my fault."

When Muriel was able to speak, she said in a small voice, "Why is it your fault, darling? It's my fault for allowing myself to become like this." She looked down at her body. "I don't blame you one minute for what you've done."

Lindquist didn't understand. She must be referring to what he had said. He was silent in guilt and misery.

"But I do think we should have a talk, Rod."

"A talk?"

"There are some things we should get straight between us." She fell limply into a chair.

"No, everything is fine now, honey," he said. "Everyone has their blowups."

"But," continued Muriel, "this isn't the time for that kind of talking. We can't be close in this awful place. Why don't we leave? We could go back to Santa Barbara. It's on the way home."

"We'll see," said Lindquist. "We'll discuss it. I think you're right. We should leave. Definitely. But not Santa Barbara. It would be better for us to go home. That's where we belong. We'll talk about it tomorrow. We'll wind the whole mess up with this party. Come on, dear, I need a drink. I need a lot of them."

"I'm sorry for my part, darling. And I love you. You'll never know how much. Now I'll fix my face and we'll go to the party."

Laura Bishop got out of the tub and began to dry herself vigorously. She had never been very conscious of her body. Perhaps that was because she had never allowed anyone else to be conscious of it. It did not relate to anyone, was an independent private thing. Her body was simply a substance of flesh and bone she carried around unmindfully, accepting it, seldom giving it more than a passing thought, or a glance in the mirror.

But now she considered her body directly. She really saw it for the first time in detail. They were nice legs. Finely molded with a crisp tapering, yet soft. Jay Humphrey had said so last night when he was . . . And her tummy was tight, nearly flat. And her breasts . . . Well, what was it he said? "My God, Laura, with a figure like this why do you hide yourself as if you were ashamed of being a woman? Why do you make like a boy in your clothes? Huh? Tell me that. Why are you hiding?" She was terribly embarrassed. And frightened, too. So that for an answer, she could only cry a little. No man had ever seen her half naked before.

Laura folded the towel neatly on the wash rack, slipped into panties and bra. She went into the bedroom and from a closet took down the white satin cocktail dress she had bought that morning in Santa Monica just for the occasion. She liked white. Half the things she owned were white—so clean. The dress had a half-moon dip of neckline, was a sheath and would reveal as much of her as possible without branding her as cheap. Her dark hair would contrast beautifully. Never again would she wear it in that off-the-face knotted manner which was so severe. Star Osborne would have a difficult time outshining her tonight!

She laid the dress on the bed carefully. Then she went to her vanity, sat on the little bench and began to do her nails, occasionally glancing up at herself in the mirror as if seeing a stranger.

It must be that this thing inside her, this antiseptic for sexual impurity she clutched so tightly, was not her own at all but an imposition from her mother. Else why did she now feel in some remote corner of awakening that sex was not quite so soiled and unnatural, not quite so violently self-destructive and evil? Was it that she half-enjoyed those clever and knowing hands with their certain exploring of her body? And was she rationalizing as her mother did, though in reverse? Oh yes, she knew, or at least sensed, that her mother rationalized herself into that dry bitter hatred of all forms of lust. And hid behind a frantic theology, using it as a weapon.

She had sensed it long ago, with the coming of awareness and intelligence. But intelligence and awareness were poorly armed in the battle with years of indoctrination

66

and habit. Especially when in a woman unexposed, mother- and self-protected, there was so little urge. There was not the man's needing, the impulsion with which the physical desire could drive through habit and mental discipline to satisfaction. No, not the man's needing which *had* to—even if it *was* wrong. And what little needing there had been soon decayed and was forgotten. But never forgotten, the incessant harping theme of her mother.

The shameful thought had come to her on occasion, as it did now, that her mother might well be avenging herself upon the only representative of her father at hand. Or that because her mother's own life was barren, she meant to hold by force of will the one endowment her father had left her. And do this by building around the child and the woman a wall of chastity so solid as to repulse any man.

If she could have believed this totally, Laura might long ago have revolted. But the one issue on which she could not stand against her mother's logic and appeal to her emotions was her father's "cruelty to his own daughter." Not once in all the years since he went down to that drugstore and slipped away into the night "with that evil woman" had her father been in touch—sent a message, phoned or written. He could at least have written. Or on her birthdays, arranged some secret meeting. With her yearning heart she would gladly have conspired. But no, he became only a faded and distorted image in her mind. Then was a void. He might as well be dead. So this was the wedge which opened her mind to the believability of all things her mother said about "carnal appetites—condemned and punished by the good Lord."

Laura curled her fingers and blew on the fresh paint of her nails. She began to brush her hair with long rhythmic strokes.

She might have gone on for years to become a gaunt and skin-parched replica of her mother, if not for Jay Humphrey. Love had made another wedge in another part of her mind. Why did she love him with his easy taking, so opposite to her dreary virtue? Why did she love him when he apparently came back to her as a cast-off of Star Osborne? She didn't know that. She didn't understand. There was only the joy of needing, really needing once in her life. The ecstasy of needing so badly you altered and changed on inward command, being what you thought you could never be—for love. Being a kind of Star Osborne for a night so that you could hold what was finally yours. But had she really been that? Had she really changed very much?

"No, I can't, Jay darling, I just can't!"

"Won't."

"No, no! I love you and I would. But even the thought is making me sick. Could you open that window? I need more air. I'm really going to be sick."

"Maybe you'd feel better if it wasn't in a car. Your apartment?"

"No, darling. It wouldn't make a bit of difference. And why risk being seen for—"

"Just petting?"

"You don't know how much it is for me. Never in my life have I—"

"I can believe that. Coming from you, I really can."

"Is that a compliment? You sound angry. Don't be angry. Be patient. Just for a little while. You'll be glad. I'll make you glad."

"Of course you will, baby. I'm sorry. I'll be patient."

"Do you love me?"

"I love them all. The big and the—"

"What? What!"

"Just kidding. I love you, baby. Like always."

"You won't leave me for—for any reason? Because I need you, need you."

"Not for any reason. Now, shall we slip back down the hill in our still white, still pure, chariot?"

"Please don't tease me."

"Sorry, baby." And then the sound of the motor . . .

So had she really changed? Yes, she had changed. A great deal! And it was only the beginning. Maybe tonight, after the party . . .

Laura finished with her hair. With tender care she put on the dress, then her make-up, and studied herself. It was a very pleasing effect. If she ever looked beautiful and—carnal—this was the time.

She went to a window and looked out. There was an oblique view of the ocean but light in the room spoiled it. She cut the light and in the darkness stood peering out. There was an absolutely full moon. Pale light, soft as a whisper, came floating down from the sky, dusting the face of the beach with a talcum whiteness, touching the

68

shoreline ocean with a silver froth, making tender shadows out of harsh structures.

This will be the first night of my life, she thought. This will be the beginning. All the dead things will drain out of me and I'll be alive, alive! Alive and needing. Full of needing. But even as she thought this, some sad knowing, a disbelief like a stealthy presence, stole upon her, reaching out a melancholy hand to choke away her joy.

Then she heard the knock. And unaware that she was still in darkness, went to answer.

two

Royce could tell in the first hour that the party was going to get out of hand. Everyone was drinking as if they had arrived late on New Year's Eve and had to catch up, had to be stoned by midnight. It was compulsive drinking—feverish brain-washing with alcohol.

Humphrey was already much more voluble than usual. And he wasn't exactly an introvert. He stood in a corner of the room where Royce was seated next to Rod and Muriel Lindquist on his right, Laura on his left. He had one foot on a red square of plastic-covered ottoman, his big frame bent forward, a drink tilted in one hand, the other holding a cigarette which waved with his gestures. Lindquist had been discoursing on the missile program, the probabilities of war, the changing techniques of battle. The conversation had narrowed down from the broader aspects to the psychological pressures and this had led Humphrey into an accounting of one or two of his own experiences in combat.

Royce was listening attentively because he had the impression that this might be a rare opportunity to learn something more intimate of the ties between Humphrey and Erickson, who was now dancing with Star Osborne in the background. But so far Humphrey had said nothing of a personal nature, had not even mentioned Erickson.

"Fear," Humphrey was saying, "it's the main ingredient of life and the main ingredient of war. Nearly everything happens because some poor bastard or a whole collection of them is afraid. And if there's another war, that's what's

69

going to get us into it, brother—fear. God-damn right. Fear!"

He spoke directly to Royce and Lindquist, including Muriel and Laura only on the periphery of his conversation with a quick lateral slashing of his eyes. Laura was bent forward slightly, her face intent, listening as though Humphrey were playing Romeo to her Juliet. Muriel was only half attentive. She seemed to know it was man-talk and her soft little smile was merely polite while her eyes roamed the room and back again.

"It's a funny thing what fear will do," said Humphrey. "A very damn funny thing. There were a lot of guys in my outfit who got wounded—big, hard-looking guys who got tagged pretty bad, but not so it should have killed them. They would stare down and they would see that god-damn wound oozing blood and they would turn a sort of sweaty gray-white in the face and sometimes they would pass out and they would be dead in maybe five minutes to an hour. Fear, that's all.

"Then there would be some little skin-and-bones character who had a wound would kill a rhino. But he would have a queer little grin on his puss and you would see life in his eyes, and hope. The bastard shouldn't live, not a prayer, but he did. You never can tell where fear is and what it'll do.

"But there was one big guy who was afraid of nothing and nobody. Maybe he didn't have sense enough to be afraid. But he died anyway. Wally Dykes, his name was. One of those slow-talking, sun-leathered Texan types. Man, you talk about big—he was capital B—Big! About six-four, I'd say. And lanky. Long arms and giant feet and hands big enough to hide a bowling ball. He was one of those square guys—square all over—face, jaw, shoulders, hams, anywhere you looked that guy was square. Even inside, he was a square Joe."

Humphrey looked around for an ashtray, found it, came back.

"Anyway, we were dug in deep this night, everyone cozy in his little hole in the ground. And then came the goddamn dawn, which no one was very happy to see, because there are a lot of cute little snipers up in those trees. And they wait just for that sun to peek over the horizon. Because they've got the same equipment and they know what's the first thing a guy has to do in the

70

morning." Humphrey's eyes performed that lateral ma-
neuver to Laura and Muriel. "Excuse me, ladies . . ."
He puffed, jiggled ice, swallowed. "So, Mr. Gook-sniper
would wait until the first GI came up for the relief job
and let him have it. Wham!

"On this particular morning the whole platoon just lay
there waiting for someone else to make the test first.
Finally Dykes said, 'Aw, the hell with it,' and got up big as
a mountain and walked over to a tree. Nothing happened.
So he ambled on back—he had a walk as lazy as his
speech—and stood over my foxhole, looking down at me
with a big grin. I had taken a forty-five from a guy who
wouldn't need it any more, and for some reason I forget, Dykes had borrowed it. He leaned about a mile down
and passed it to me. 'Cleaned it nice and pretty for you,'
he said. I looked at it, took out the clip and noticed that
it had a speck of rust on it. 'You get tired when you came
to this clip?' I said, joking. 'There's a spot on it, soldier—
two days' K.P.'

" 'Fork it over,' he said, still grinning, and I did. He
stood there like the Eiffel Tower and began to wipe it
with a rag from his pocket. 'Better come down in out of
the clouds,' I said. 'Some gook might have you in mind
for a hair cut.' But he just shook his head and went on
wiping.

"I don't remember if I heard the shot. But next thing
you know he flinched, no more than if a bee had stung
him right over the heart where that little hole was beginning to blush red. Maybe the smile faded a little but his
expression didn't change much at all. And listen to this.
For about three or four seconds *he went right on wiping
that clip.* Then he leaned down as polite as could be and
passed it to me. And at that moment when his face was
so close to mine, it did change, but no more than a little
bit of a wince. 'Move over,' he said. 'I've been hit.' So I
scrunched over real quick and he lay down almost on top
of me and his eyes never closed but he was dead. Now
there was a man! Anyone else would have folded right up
and been cold before he touched ground. I'm telling you,
I damn near broke down and cried."

While Lindquist was shaking his head solemnly and
Royce was forming a question which would bring Erickson
into the war picture, Humphrey set down his glass,
mashed his cigarette, said, "C'mon, Laura, on your feet,

71

gal. Let's dance." They swirled away to join Star and Erickson on the floor. Lindquist and his wife followed suit and Royce was left alone.

A shaggy white rug had been pulled back and the couples danced on the hardwood floor to music from a portable radio. In the dining alcove a cloth-covered table had been set up with an assortment of bottles, glasses and cold cuts. Ice cubes brimmed from kitchen bowls. It was strictly a buffet, help-yourself arrangement—and no one was bashful. There was every kind of liquor from Scotch to gin and a variety of mixes. In the center of the table was a large turkey and a gleaming set of carving tools. The turkey, thought Royce, had probably come from a delicatessen. But Star had gone to a bit of expense, if not trouble.

Yet, as if to deny her hospitality, she made no attempt to mingle with the guests as a group, or play hostess. It was as if she had provided the place and the necessary equipment for a party, then said, The hell with it, entertain yourselves. Or as if she had brought the force of certain personalities together to see how they would react upon each other. Her very presence was a catalyst. She did not have to organize or assume command. Watching her, Royce was as confused as ever. There had to be something more purposeful to Star Osborne's action than this switch-partners, love-it-up-and-see-what-happens kick. Any such plan must involve some benefit to her. But what benefit evaded him completely.

She was dressed in a burgundy taffeta, a strapless gown cut so low that the white cream of her bosom seemed in danger of spilling out of it altogether with the slightest exertion. Even Laura Bishop's plunging satin was modest by comparsion.

Humphrey and Erickson danced with their partners in the same corner of the room—almost back to broad back at this moment when there was so little movement to the slow rhythm. In the semi-darkness they were tall shadows cut out of the same pattern, lithe animals with panther grace, brush-cut twins with strong clean profiles bent to look into the faces of their partners. Yet, though they danced near, there was now an aura of distance between them, a separateness that was noticeable to Royce only in contrast to their former unity.

Did Lindquist feel it, too? Over Muriel's shoulder he

72

watched them with a curious expression.

There was a pause in the music, the drone of the announcer, and then the furious beat of a mambo. Star came to life in Erickson's arms. Her feet flew in quick rhythm and perfect coordination. Her high buttocks waved, her body writhed in a sinuous interpretation so daring and sensual Royce could think only of the horizontal implications. It was dancing in the finest sense, and yet it was a stark ritual to the goddess—sex. Star Osborne was the goddess, making sex visible in all its tempting evil, the dance like a hymn of praise to consummation.

She was too fast and too skilled for Erickson. In the end he was forced to merely shift his feet in one spot, a foil for her abandon. Essentially she was alone on the floor. And all stood aside and watched with mixed emotions—female shock, male fascination. Her hips undulated, breasts heaved, long hair swished across bronze shoulders. Tick-a-tack-tick-tack—tick-a-tack-tick-tack! went the music. And then with a crash and a squeal, it was over.

Star stood still for a trance-like moment as there followed a smattering of applause. Glancing around the room with a self-complacent smile, she made a little bow and sat down, leaving Erickson to follow her or not. He followed.

Lindquist had been watching Star with such intense awe, he had to be guided off the floor by Muriel. Laura's mouth was open, her head cocked a little, as if she had heard something which didn't sound quite right. Humphrey, smiling a knowing smile and, tongue in cheek, led her into the new dance. It came to Royce that of them all, only Humphrey understood the frantic churning within Star Osborne. But what was it he understood?

Shortly after midnight the trouble began. At this point everyone appeared wildly or morosely saturated in alcohol, according to their mood and personality. Star and Humphrey were especially gay with Laura and Erickson hard on their heels. Royce felt that he was somewhere in the middle. Muriel and Rod Lindquist were sullen or just quiet, though Muriel always looked a little withdrawn and preoccupied.

It had been obvious to Royce for some time that Star was flirting outrageously, if obliquely, with Lindquist. This was the last male outpost, still unconquered, and all her willful energy was concentrated in that direction. Royce

73

could tell by the set of her chin that nothing could or would stop her.

Every time Lindquist looked up, Royce noticed that her smile captured him from some corner of the room. A cat smile below narrowed eyes, cold and certain, it teased and tempted, seemed to hover in the air even when she had turned her head. Lindquist fidgeted uncomfortably, glancing at his wife.

Sometimes Star was more direct. She would swivel across the room, bringing her musky animality, and ask Lindquist to dance. He always refused for one reason or another. He didn't dance well at all, he was tired, he was too loaded.

He finally did dance with her, probably to get her off his neck. Or because of the incident which embarrassed, flustered or—who knows?—excited him.

She had been sitting directly across from Lindquist on a sofa, chatting inattentively with Erickson. Muriel had gone to the buffet table and was gorging herself with turkey, washing it down with rum and cola. Royce sat alone with Lindquist and he saw.

Star had uncrossed her legs as she talked to Erickson, absently weaving them apart and together again as she leaned indolently back. Suddenly she lifted one leg higher than seemed necessary and scissored it across the other. As she did this, her skirt came up and there was the flash of rich thighs altogether exposed. And where there should have been panties, she was naked. Primly she smoothed back her skirt, then looked directly across at Lindquist and boldly smiled.

Out of the corner of his eye, Royce saw Lindquist redden. He threw a darting glance at Royce to see if he had noticed. Royce looked straight ahead and kept a poker face.

In a moment, Star gave Erickson a pat on his crew-cut crown and came over, staggering slightly. "Sir," she said. "Sir Rod Lindquist, you look so glum. Won't you have one little dance with me and I promise never to mention it again. Please?"

Lindquist sighed and reluctantly, unsteadily, got to his feet. Star gave him a smile of acute satisfaction and danced him away. Erickson watched but did not seem to mind. It was almost as if he tolerated this deference to

74

an "older man," a married man who would never in any way be competition.

Now Muriel returned, chewing, chewing and washing down with her drink. She observed the dancing of her husband with Star in a clinical abstract way. At least that was the impression she gave. She said nothing. Meanwhile there was no daylight or any other light between Star and Lindquist. Her big warm body had the look of devouring his frail one. As they danced, she whispered in his ear, chuckling, throwing her head back, chuckling again deep in her throat. Then her face changed and she appeared to make some serious plea to which Lindquist gave his head a shake of negation. She spoke again with a trace of smile and he shrugged his shoulders. Arm in arm they walked toward the kitchen and disappeared behind the door.

Muriel felt the tension mounting in her like a high thin scream. She knew all along this was going to happen. It had to. It was just a question of when and how. She swallowed and the fragments went down with a dry clinging to her throat. She took a long gulp of the rum cola, conscious that Royce and some of the others were watching her covertly. For a good minute, she sat perfectly still, trying to stare right through the kitchen door. She put the drink down on the table deliberately then, standing with her shoulders back, walked proudly, regally, to the kitchen, allowing not the least emotion to show on her face.

She opened the door and stepped in, closing it behind her.

The woman was leaning back against the kitchen table and Rod was bent over her, kissing her shoulder in a descending path. On her husband's face was the most rapacious of looks—an almost snarling savagery. On the woman's face as she watched the downward progress of Rod's lips, was an expression of such utter victory it was like the climax of passion.

Star Osborne turned and saw Muriel. She made no move to push Rod away. On the contrary, she held his head tightly against her. Now her expression said, You see, they all come to me sooner or later on bended knee. Married or single they must, for I am irresistible. I am desire itself.

75

Rod must have felt her presence. His head swung slowly about. His mouth fell open, he jerked upright but was unable to speak.

"You whore," said Muriel softly. "You nymphomaniac bitch. Your time is coming, you monster."

She looked at Rod. "And now this," she said under tears. "And now this." She turned and as sedately as she had come, she went out and crossed the living room.

She didn't want to leave in an obvious huff. To stall, she placed a mechanical little smile on her face and made for the buffet table. She stood for a moment looking at the fat repulsive turkey. She picked up the carving knife and studied the long blade. She had a picture of Rod's back as he bent over that monster. It was his fault, really. He should know better than to humiliate her in front of all these people. And now he had made her whole reason for the vacation a hideous joke. She lifted the knife and saw it come down and sink to the haft in his back, the most astonishing look of the betrayed on his face.

Someone touched her arm. She turned with the knife. It was Rod, wiping lipstick onto the back of his hand. "Come on, Muriel," he said gruffly and loudly to her and to the room at large. "I just wanted to see what all the god-damn fuss was about. Nothing. A god-damn soiled, used up, second-hand bag. Nothing! I'm sorry, honey," he said more softly. "Now let's go to bed."

Muriel put down the knife. It seemed a great effort. Then she followed Rod out the front door, the laughter of that woman from the kitchen doorway trailing them into the darkness.

three

Royce gazed disgustedly at Star as she came out of the kitchen. She was pointing at the door which had just closed behind Rod and Muriel. She was giggling. "If you could have seen . . ." she said to no one. "The look on her face—like a wounded buffalo. And I was just having a little fun."

All except Humphrey had serious unresponsive faces. But Humphrey wore his knowing acidic smile. Seeing him

76

somehow as her one ally, she went toward him. He got up and they danced.

Immediately Laura's face closed like a hard smooth stone and she came to sit beside Royce. Her eyes flicked over Star dancing with her lover and she said in a strained voice, "Tell me, Stan, is she beautiful? So much more attractive than I am?"

Royce considered the question honestly. "No," he said. "I don't think she's particularly beautiful. As for attraction—well, yes. She has a flamboyant, devastating kind of pull for a man. Until you get to know her, what you *can* know of her. Then, if she doesn't have a hold on you, you turn away with loathing and you take another look at Laura Bishop. And you say to yourself, this Laura Bishop is really a very pretty and charming girl. Much more attractive than Star Osborne."

"Thanks, Stan. That was a very sweet thing to say."

"No, it wasn't sweet at all. It was honest. I meant it."

She looked at him as if seeing him for the first time. "I think you do mean it," she said. "You give the impression of being terribly sincere. We should have a long talk sometime. But right now—well—I just don't know what to do about her."

"Don't do anything," said Royce. "She burns for a man with a big bright flame. But when the flame goes out he'll be able to see again. Meanwhile just be yourself and wait. I'm going to break it up. Besides, I have something to say to our friend."

He rose over Laura's objections and tapped Humphrey's arm. The aggressive look on Humphrey's face altered to one of surprise when he turned and saw that it was Royce. "I shall abdicate," he said with mock solemnity. "But temporarily. I shall return." He departed.

"So," said Star, "the prodigal comes home. After many a cold winter. I've been expecting you."

Royce danced her to a corner of the room. "All right," he said. "You've made the rounds. You've had us all. Now does it end? Or do you start all over?"

"It began with you, didn't it, darling? So logically it should come back to you."

"Never. I've seen too much."

"I don't think so, Stanley."

"Listen," he hissed in her ear. "You've got a lot of basically decent people at each other's throats. You've

77

had your fun. So now why don't you pack your witch's bag of tricks and steal away before dawn. Go crawl back into the same cesspool that spawned you."

"You bastard. I won't leave, you know. I'll still be here tomorrow trying not to laugh right out loud. Yes, you're a bastard, Stanley darling. But I still have a certain yen for you. I'd like to kill you with my own little weapon. Why don't we go for a ride, Stanley? Far up into the hills. Some of the excitement went out the door with fat Muriel. I'm bored silly. How about it?"

"Not with you."

"Then I'll just have to find someone else."

"If you're not gone in the morning—"

"What then?"

"I don't know," said Royce. "But I'll think about it. I'm going to spend a long time thinking about it."

Humphrey's bulk appeared beside them. "I have returned," he said.

At first it appeared to Erickson that his earlier sense of uneasiness about the party had been unfounded. Star had remained close by his side and as attentive as if they were —man and wife. Yes, the thought had come to him that they might very well be man and wife. In fact this uneasiness produced by Humphrey's insinuations had goaded him into thinking that before the night was over, he would ask Star to marry him. He would get Star aside and she would hug him with gratitude and affection. Then perhaps he would call for quiet and in the dramatic silence which followed, would make the announcement. There would be much hand-shaking and slapping on the back and Star's swelling red dress would not be an invitation but a banner on which would be written in the invisible but indelible ink of social ethics: This is the property of Bruce Erickson—hands off.

But the opportunity had not presented itself and, further, his fears had been grounded. The party was slowly coming unglued, disintegrating at the core and becoming something loose and sordid.

When Lindquist came out embarrassed, smudged with lipstick, fouling Star's name in an attempt to save face, the incident left a very bad taste in his mouth. He had wanted to cream Lindquist with a single blow to his smeared delicate features, shut his dirty mouth. But this

78

would seem like a childish admission of his own insecurity, and anyway Lindquist was half-shot and just trying to cover himself with his wife. So he pretended not to hear. But his mood of gaiety had faded and his plans had gone sour.

Next thing you know Jay was dancing with Star, holding her too close and talking in that intimate and conspiratorial way which literally frightened him. Because Star seemed to enjoy it, to be a party to it.

Then Royce cut in, but Royce seemed angry and that took the sting out of any possibility there. But why was Royce angry? Then Jay was right back again breaking it up with that condescending smile, hard, possessive. Who the hell did he think he was? God-damn. God-damn! And cutting in just at the moment when he was going to take Star outside for a few minutes and have that talk with her.

Now they were dancing with that same molding intimacy, touching everywhere. Those lips smiling—wide, moist and soft—soft. Hair sways long and perfumed across her back. Her back. He could feel his hands running down it to the little hollow before the smooth abrupt arching. Only last. . . Damn! Oh, god-damn him! Doesn't he understand that I love her more than he could ever love anyone? To him she's just another babe. Out of hundreds. But to me, the only one. My God, the two of us. Never to be alone. Lonely, lonely. That's me, a lonely sonofabitch.

You think he cares? Huh! He doesn't give a damn. His fun, his kicks first. Never was a friend. Never really was a friend at all. Looking out for number one. All along looking out for number one.

And now Humphrey was guiding her over to the buffet and they were inspecting the bottles, holding up some empties. They tried to stand flat-footed, but couldn't—kept swaying a little. Drunk. Well, maybe that was it—drunk. He shouldn't be such a wet-nurse, worry baby.

Humphrey said something and she looked at him and began to nod slowly, biting her lip as though to keep from smiling. After which Humphrey stepped away from her to a corner of the table and, squinting at the bottles, began to write swiftly on a piece of paper, an envelope he had taken with a pen from his pocket. He tore that portion from the envelope and folded it, holding it in his hand, stuffing the rest in his pocket. Then he took Star's arm and they came right toward him.

"Listen, buddy boy," he said thickly. "We're about cleaned of hootch. Star knows a bar just down the road. If the right guy is on duty we can replenish the stock." He looked down at the piece of paper in his hand meaningfully and with an oddly secret implication, as if to draw attention to it. "Now I've got a little list here and if we slip this guy a few bucks extra, why he'll fill it like a prescription. Just what the doctor ordered."

"We need more booze like we need a bonfire in here," said Erickson. He didn't know exactly what was happening but felt there was something sneaky and wrong.

"Gotta keep the guests happy," said Humphrey with finality.

"I'll go with you," said Erickson.

"Nah," said Humphrey. "Anyone else leaves, you won't have a god-damn party. Won't take five, ten minutes. Right back."

Erickson wanted to make an issue. But Star was looking at him speculatively, a trace of scorn in her eyes. It was as though she challenged his trust, even his manhood. Her eyes dared him to be jealous and take the consequences.

"Okay," he said. "Go ahead. Bring some butts, too. I'm almost out."

Star's expression restored him. "Wait for me, sweetie. We'll hurry." She moved toward the door.

The instant her back was turned Humphrey tossed the piece of paper which was folded in the palm of his hand. It fell squarely in Erickson's lap and, as he picked it up, Humphrey gave him a broad wink and was gone out the door with Star.

Erickson unfolded the paper and read Jay's scrawl:

> To watch Old Faithful in action, wait ten
> minutes. Then turn left on beach, walk
> until you hear voices—or see things!
> Sneak—as in night patrol.
>
> This is a sure cure for a sick, sick
> lover. Don't miss it!

Erickson felt as if all the juices of his body had drained out of him. He read the note again. Then he sat staring

80

at it without seeing it at all. Finally he crumpled it into a tiny ball and flung it angrily away from him. It struck the wall and bounced into a corner of the room.

He looked at his watch.

Laura Bishop saw the whole thing. She was furious because Jay Humphrey did not have the common courtesy to walk across the room and tell her he was going out on some errand. Or the pretense of an errand. With Star Osborne, if there was a real errand it would manage to get side-tracked anyway. Was this just the catty distorted thought of jealousy? It was possible that Jay was perfectly honest and merely thoughtless. He had been checking the liquor supply and writing something down on a piece of paper.

But wasn't that the same piece of paper he tossed in Bruce Erickson's lap? Why would he do that unless . . .?

Next to her, Stan Royce was saying, "Dance, Laura?"

"No thanks. Not just now. Excuse me a minute, Stan?"

She got up and pretended to go to the john. But when she got to the bedroom where there was a single lamp burning weakly, she just sat on the bed a few minutes, staring at her shoes in the gloom, her thoughts swift and anxious. Then she went back into the living room. Avoiding Stan's gaze, she walked to a corner of the big picture window and stared out to where moonlight spilled brightly over beach and water.

She looked down and to the right. The little ball of paper rested a few inches from the corner where she had seen Bruce hurl it as though it were some obscene limerick too disgusting to keep. She wanted desperately to pick it up. But Bruce sat sternly in his chair only a few feet away. She waited another minute, trying to decide how to veil her movements.

She was edging toward the paper, intending to kick it with her foot, when Bruce got up suddenly and stalked out the door. She looked around the room and was amazed to see that she and Stan Royce were now the only ones remaining. Everyone had just vanished into the night, a stealthy kind of departure. She felt frightened and alone. The radio, blaring stridently, filled the room with raucous jazz and made it seem still more empty. It was somehow like a carnival from which all the people had fled, the music still echoing sadly, the carousel still whirling her around, but all the people gone.

81

Stan Royce was looking her directly in the eye. Though the music crashed, for seconds the silence between them was frozen solid. His clear soft eyes were warm and on his face was an expression of immeasurable sympathy.

"I'm not sure if it would be wise for you to pick it up," he said finally.

She stood for another eternity looking into his eyes. "I have to."

"Well then, if you must—"

She bent down and the paper was in her hand. She twisted it open and read, looked up at Stan, read it again. She came to stand next to his chair with the note still open. She held it not quite extended toward him. "I'd rather not show it to you," she said hoarsely.

He smiled a little. "I have no need to see it."

She crumpled the paper, opened her purse and dropped the note inside. "I hate to leave you alone, Stan. But if you don't mind, I'll go to bed. The party seems to have just died without anyone but us to bury it. But I'm sure the others will be back in a few minutes. Do you mind?"

He stood up. "I don't mind," he said. "It never was a party anyway. It was just a scramble in a cage." He took her hand between both of his. His face became set. A muscle of his jaw twitched. "Go to bed and don't think," he said. "Make a big black hole and just fall into it. In the morning you'll find everything will be different. Something has to be done and I guess I'm elected. We can't all be bystanders. Tomorrow there'll be a change. I promise you."

"No," she said. "It's not ever going to change. But I'm glad to know you, Stan. Really know you. I think you're one of the kindest men I've ever met. Good night, Stan."

She kissed him quickly on the mouth and went out the door.

Erickson trudged along in the sand, peering ahead. The moon was a pale-blue beacon in the sky and visibility was good. Still, he could see nothing but the arid beach, hear nothing but the empty smashing of waves. There was a hollow rushing in his ears and sound came as if heard from the bottom of a deep well. The night was intensely beautiful—soft and shadowy quiet.

A soggy wretchedness was in him but hard anger had not yet overcome him. It might be only another of

82

Humphrey's filthy jokes that at any other time would be worthy of just a shrug and a bitter laugh. That's Jay Humphrey. But the note had overtones of clever planning and there had been the earlier threat . . . Though he despised himself for it, he would have to follow through.

He did not hear anything at all but came to the place so suddenly he almost fell down the gully on top of them. He pulled up sharply, gulped air and stopped his breathing.

He could see them clearly. Their clothes had been spread out beneath them and their naked bodies shone like polished statuary, alabaster dummies entwined and rigid in a moment of time—until they came to life and the grotesque horror went on and on. Until he could hear the shouting inside him. Stop—stop—stop! And then they did stop with a little sobbing sound and fell apart like loathsome spiders. And he turned and walked back without knowing where he walked and in what direction.

Laura Bishop closed the door and looked to see if Stan might be watching from the window. He wasn't. She went out to the beach. Of course when the note said left, it must mean left as you faced the water. She made the turn, stopped and removed her high-heeled shoes. Carrying them in her hand, she scurried forward quickly, lest she change her mind.

She saw Bruce Erickson coming toward her at some distance. His head was bent, he seemed oblivious. He must be coming back. She ran up the beach from him toward the highway and fell prone, waiting until he passed. Then she went back and found his footsteps, followed them.

She heard the giggling first and when she crept up to the edge of the depression, they were standing naked and embracing. Then they began to dress. She ran from the sight of them—fast—as if she could run swiftly enough to escape it altogether. She circled the building and approached it from the highway side, sneaking up to her apartment.

Once inside she did not turn on the light but went to the window. The pale moonlight had a look of utter coldness, a lonely iceberg floating in the sky. Shivering, she glanced at the sweaty palms of her hands. They seemed to her darkly stained and slimy. She pressed them against

83

her and slowly begin to wipe them across the front of her new dress.

Bruce Erickson might have gone right on past the Tides. But out of the corner of his eye he caught the shine of something in the moonlight. It was the green enamel luster which radiated from the hull of the boat. The bow had not been shoved entirely under the porch and protruded visibly.

Erickson paused, stared at the boat. The sight of it set off another rocket of anger. Fury had been bursting inside him in stages, as missiles which soar in a rush of fading power, only to fire themselves anew.

He hated the boat. Hated the god-damn thing! Seeing the shine and polish of it which he had once brought about with loving hands, he hated it. And hating it, the remembered gleam of steel sitting in his mind, he went around to the side of the building. The big long-handled ax was in the shed where they kept the cord wood to feed the fireplaces on cool damp nights. He grabbed it and plowed with long strides back to the boat. He dropped the ax and loosed the lines fore and aft. He removed the tarp. Then with much sweating but the strength of blind rage, he caught the boat by the chrome lifting handle forward and slowly pulled it from under the porch.

Now he picked up the ax again and with powerful high-swinging but frantic blows, chopped and hammered alternately. It was a difficult task because the Fiberglas was strong and resisted destruction. But finally he accomplished a broken and battered shambles.

A small part of his anger diminished with the exertion and sweet satisfaction, just enough to allow him to think for a moment. When they came back, Humphrey would see the boat and stop dead with shock. So now he hurled the ax in the rubble of scattered gear and stole under the porch to wait in the darkness.

In less than five minutes he heard voices becoming increasingly audible over the wash of waves.

". . . ought to at least make it look good . . . might be able to get a bottle or two and—" Star's voice, then Humphrey's, louder.

"Nah. No sense in that. Just say we didn't have any luck. I'm pooped."

Laughter by Star, mocking and full of implication. Then

84

silence and the soft approaching swish of feet in sand.

"Jesus, God! Christ almighty! My boat, my boat! Beat all to hell. God-damn. Who would do a thing like that?"

Erickson stepped from behind a beam into full moonlight. "I would," he said.

All stood monument-still. There was an aching timeless gap. Then Humphrey moved closer, craning his neck. "Bruce! F'chrissake! You didn't. Why would you? Why!" Another silence. "Aw well, now listen, kid. It was for your own good. Cool off and think about it. There wasn't any other way. The old cure. Now you know."

"Now I know. You were jealous, Humphrey. For once I took something out of your slimy hands and you wanted it back. But the scheme didn't work, you filthy, filthy bastard. It backfired. You stink, Humphrey. I can smell you. I can smell you dead."

From a corner of his vision he had a glimpse of Star. Her lips were spread in a grimace of approval. He could not see her eyes clearly but her attitude of tense waiting, the expression on her face, was of utter fascination.

Crouching slightly, he began to creep forward.

four

As soon as Laura had gone, Royce made himself a drink and began to pace the living room. He knew from Laura's reaction to the note, from Erickson's face when he went out the door, the subtle frictions were over. The real trouble, the violent purpose of some twisted plan was fused. He had to stop Star Osborne. But how? How! Warnings, threats, insults were pebbles against that fortress of determination.

He stood still in the center of the room. He looked around him. His eyes came to rest on the little hall that led to the bedroom. He set down the drink and went to the front door, opened it. He listened. He closed the door and hurried into the bedroom. The light was dim but it would have to do. He bent over the dresser and began searching among the expensive scented garments.

In a bottom drawer he came across a purse, opened it. There was a finely tooled, handsome wallet. It was

85

crammed with currency—large bills. There was a driver's license bearing her name and other identification, all with a Cleveland address. He studied the wallet and recognized what was supposed to be a secret compartment. In it was a newspaper clipping, Cleveland dateline. He took it to the light and began to read with astonishment.

He was folding the clipping and putting it in his pocket when he heard the sounds. There was a rhythmic pounding and splintering which seemed to come from under the building. He tried to place it, understand its meaning. Distant and muffled, it throbbed beneath him. Quickly he returned the wallet to the purse and the purse to the drawer, closing it. He looked and everything was in order.

He went swiftly to the living room and turned down the radio. There was a single thud which now reached him clearly, then a clatter of metal. All sound ceased. He found his drink and sipped at it a while, thinking about the clipping. Then he heard raised voices and went out the door to the beach.

Standing just behind a corner of the building, Royce got the picture in a glance—the wreck of the boat, the strange expectant look of Star Osborne, Erickson, shoulders bunched, advancing on Humphrey with a quiet and deadly stealth while Humphrey stood tall and waiting, arms loose at his sides.

"Don't try it, Bruce," said Humphrey. "You'd only get hurt and we'd both be sorry. This tramp isn't worth it."

Erickson crept upon him without reply. At that moment, Royce was thinking that there was nothing more violent than the weld of friendship broken and turned to hatred. The force of hate had subjective heat which gathered power from the very personal elements which had produced its opposite.

Erickson seemed confused when he came within striking distance of Humphrey. Because Humphrey made all his crouching caution seem ridiculous. He merely stood unguarded and waiting, making his unprotected stance a testimony to the foolishness of such a battle, the rebuke of maturity.

But after a moment's hesitation, Erickson struck him anyway—a brutal smash to the side of Humphrey's jaw which sent him reeling backwards. The contact appeared to detonate the frenzy inside Erickson for he rushed the advantage with quick jabbing blows which pummeled

86

Humphrey to the sand. Erickson had gone crazy because now he began to kick at Humphrey's body and then to stamp at his groin. But Humphrey had scissored his legs and was rolling. He had come to his knees when Erickson pulled back his foot to launch a kick that would crush his face.

But now Humphrey was alerted and with a flip was out of the way and on his feet. His former resignation, born of hope that if he took a few hits the storm would blow out, was gone. He stood, head down in boxing position, left extended, presenting a minimum target. His attention was fixed and purposeful.

Tall graceful shadows in the moonlight, so alike in silhouette they might be fighting alter egos, they danced around each other. Twisting, jabbing, feinting for an opening, there was the look about them of professional skill.

But the tortured thing in Erickson had no time or patience with cleverness and skill. He came in a windmilling rush at Humphrey, delivering a flurry of damaging but indecisive blows. Humphrey danced back a step or two, his long left flashed in with a flat meaty sound and blood gushed from Erickson's nose. When Erickson came with another flurry, the precise hammer of Humphrey's fist made a crimson smear across his mouth.

They were vicious and careful blows but not meant to cripple, only to convince. There was a confidence and accuracy in Humphrey's timing that was frightening. Yet he had to puff one of Erickson's eyes closed, open a cheek at the knob of bone, cut a flap in one lip and batter that jaw into loose rubbery submission before Erickson went down and rolled over, sobbing into the sand.

Blood dripping from his face, Humphrey stood over him. His features were contorted with pain—not physical suffering but mental anguish. He looked down and spread his hands in a gesture of helplessness. "My God, my God," he pleaded. "Oh Jesus, God."

He leaned down and gently rolled Erickson over, peering into his raw bloody face, ineffectually brushing sand from the wounds with his handkerchief. "I'm sorry, kid," he moaned. "Jesus Christ, forgive me. I couldn't help it."

Royce looked at Star Osborne. Her face was emotionless, cold. Poised as stone, she watched with narrowed eyes. Humphrey was hoisting Erickson to a sitting position. Suddenly Erickon doubled his legs and rammed Humphrey back and over. Then he got up, weaving and stumbling toward the boat. When he came back, the ax was lifted in his hands. Humphrey was just getting to his feet.

Erickson moved in and raised the ax higher.

Humphrey was on his feet. If he was afraid, it was impossible to tell. He stood fast. "I don't think you'll do it, Bruce." His voice was still pleading. "There's more between us than you'll ever have with this whore."

That was when the ax descended over Humphrey's head. But Royce was already on the run and his very momentum carried Erickson down. The ax flew out of his hands. Royce crawled over him, pinned his arms with his knees, grabbed wrists and held firm.

"All right, Humphrey," said Royce. "I'll take care of him. Now beat it before someone gets killed. Stay away from him. Let it cool till morning."

"He'll never see morning!" Erickson spat.

Humphrey gazed at him silently, winced and turned. He caught sight of Star. His mouth worked, he went up to her. "You whore," he said. "See what you've done!" His mouth worked again and he spat in her face. He pivoted and strode off.

"You go near him and I'll belt you myself," said Royce to Erickson. "So don't try. Now let's get that face cleaned up."

Erickson stood. Blood coursed from his mouth down the lapel of his jacket. He gave one long look to Star Osborne. Just a look. There was nothing in his face. Then he began to lope away around the side of the building.

Royce followed. He heard the whir of a starter and paused. In a moment Erickson had backed out furiously and careened into the night.

Royce went back. Star Osborne stood there, wiping spittle from her face. "They'll get over it," she said. "I'll help them patch it tomorrow."

Royce felt the clipping in his pocket. "No you won't," he said. "Not tomorrow or any other time."

He took her arm roughly and shoved her forward. He opened the door and closed it behind them. Inside her apartment, lights still blazed, the radio pulsed vaguely, but the rooms were deserted. For a moment he stood staring around and then pointedly at her.

"Well," he said. "I guess the party's over."

88

five

    Royce slept late the next morning and remained in his apartment reading until mid-afternoon. Occasionally he looked out the window but did not see a single one of the vacationers on the beach. It was not a pleasant day. Dirty gray clouds hung low in the sky, obscuring the sun, a damp wind blew off a choppy sea. An unusual and depressing quiet pervaded the atmosphere of the Pacific Tides. In spite of the weather it seemed unnatural to Royce that everyone should remain indoors—until he remembered the party. Then he wondered if in this place at this time there ever would be a semblance of collective spirit. He didn't think so. And since what little joy there had been for him in the vacation had been dissipated, Royce now wished he could be gone. And yet there was still this thing to be finished.

    Just before three, there was a jagged hole in the sky and the sun made a brief appearance. With it came Laura Bishop to the beach in her white bathing suit. Royce saw her carrying a robe and a book under her arm. The soft swirl was gone from her dark hair which had again been drawn back severely and tied in a knot at the nape of her neck. She moved slowly and with head and shoulders bent, looking neither right nor left. It was as if she purposely avoided so much as a glance at the other apartments and, at the same time, hoped that her progress to a spot removed from the building was unobserved. Royce changed into his trunks and, taking a towel, went out to the beach himself.

    In passing he noticed that nothing had been done about the little green boat. Torn and battered, agape with holes, it lay neglected in the sun, a sad reminder of the night's cruelties. The twisted tarp was bunched by the broken bow, fishing gear and oars lay in the welter of smashed seats and bent controls on the deck. Royce was tempted to cover the wreckage with the tarp as he would some mortal carnage. But this seemed a ridiculous sentiment on his part and with a shake of the head he turned away.

89

He did not want to intrude upon Laura if she needed to be alone. On the other hand he felt that she was not attempting to seclude herself from him particularly and she might have some information he was lacking. As a compromise he walked to a position not far from her and stood looking out to sea.

"Hello, Stan," she called. "We seem to be the only ones about."

He walked over and dropped his towel beside her. He sat down. "Do they hide from shame or the weather?" he said.

"A little of both, I imagine." There was a taint of bitterness in her smile. Her eyes were invisible behind sun glasses.

"Then you know the gruesome details?"

"I had trouble getting to sleep," she said. "I heard the commotion and looked out. This morning I saw the boat. Bruce, wasn't it?" She removed the glasses and her eyes were puffed and red-rimmed.

"It was Bruce who wrecked the boat, if that's what you mean."

"Did that start the fight?"

"No. But whatever made him smash the boat did."

"You were there?"

"Yes."

"And you stopped it?"

"Only when it got dangerous. Before that, I figured it might be better for Bruce to valve-off some steam. But I was wrong. He didn't get over it. Have you seen him?"

She nodded. "Early this morning. He was a sickening mess. He went off in his car and came back with his face bandaged."

"He went off in his car? Then he must have come back last night. And stayed in the apartment with Humphrey."

She shook her head. "I don't think he was with Jay. Maybe he slept in the car. Or on the beach. He wore the same clothes and they were a sight. I heard him and then I saw him because the car port is right below me. When he came back I looked out to see where he would go. I wondered if they had made up. He didn't go to their apartment. It was the strangest thing. He went to that little vacant room right beneath mine. He opened the door with a key and he's been there ever since, far as I know."

"He had a key?"

90

"Yes."

"Then he must have made some arrangement with Macklin. What reason would he give Macklin? And how would he explain his face? My God. I never saw two guys who were closer in my life. And now look at them."

Laura bit her lip. She seemed on the verge of tears. "It's hideous," she said. "Why would Jay do a savage thing like that—beat up his best friend?"

"He didn't want to, Laura. He did everything to avoid it. Bruce didn't leave him any choice. I think Jay is heartbroken about it."

Laura looked away. "This place has turned into a jungle," she said. "All because of one person. I think she's insane. I really do. It's as if she came here with that one perverted idea—to make trouble. Why? Who is she? No one knows the first thing about her past. She might be some—some criminal. If only she would just—"

"Leave?"

"Yes."

"I think she will. Tonight."

Laura sat up suddenly. "You know something? For heaven's sake tell me! Why will she leave?"

Her hand gripped his arm until the nails dug his flesh. He took the hand away gently, held it and squeezed. She was so tense, so strained. "Laura," he said. "There are so many things I can't tell you—now. And that's one of them. Just be calm. Everything will be all right. When she's gone, we'll have a long talk."

Her eyes were moist. "Stan, why do I care about him when there are people like you?"

"Why does Bruce care about Star? It's the same kind of foreign attraction."

She was looking over his shoulder. He followed her gaze. Muriel Lindquist had come out to the beach, dressed in a playsuit and sneakers. On Muriel, it was not exactly a becoming costume. Bewildered, she stood looking at the ruins that had once been a tidy little boat.

Laura got up, hauling the robe with her. "I think I'll go in, Stan," she said. "They'll all be out here soon and I just don't feel like talking."

"Later, then. I'll keep you posted."

"Later," she said, hesitating. There was an expression of uncertainty on her face. "By the way, Stan. You haven't seen Jay around, have you?"

"No. I haven't seen anyone but you and Muriel."

"Just wondering." She was trying desperately to sound casual while biting her lip. "I can't understand why he hasn't come out. Well, 'bye, Stan. And thanks. Knock on my door if there's anything."

"I will, Laura."

She nodded and began to move off in a dream-like walk, then turned. "No sign of Star, either?"

"No sign."

She frowned. "Just wondering," she repeated lamely and departed.

When Royce looked again, Muriel Lindquist was a solitary figure far up the beach.

Just after dark, when he was dressed and on his way to the Malibu Inn for supper, Royce stopped outside Star Osborne's door. The apartment was dark. It's time enough, he thought. He looked around and there was no one about.

He knocked on the door loudly. She didn't come and he knocked again, repeatedly. He tried the knob and the door opened. He went in and groped until he found the wall switch.

The living room was as messy as it had been when the guests deserted it. Ashtrays overflowed, there was a butt on the carpet, trampled and shredded. Cocktail and high-ball glasses with their dregs sat in ring stains on tables next to plates containing soggy scraps of food. There was a confusion of bottles on the buffet table, the turkey lay dry and exposed. There was a stench of stale tobacco and liquor.

Royce closed the door and moved across the room, paused, listened. The silence was uninhabited. There was the feeling of emptiness. He went through the little hall to the bedroom where he had found the clipping. The door was open and there was the same kind of silence. He stepped in and flicked the switch. A glare of light sprang from the ceiling fixture.

Royce stood rigid for a long time. The sight wasn't believable. It was too macabre. At first he thought he was going to be all right. He was going to walk out and get some air and assimilate it slowly, then come back in. But as he turned to leave, he was suddenly convulsed. His stomach gave a queer little twist, then heaved mightily.

He ran for the bathroom with his hand over his mouth. When he brushed against the sink, he leaned and threw up. He ran water into the basin and splashed his face. He groped for a towel and dried himself, not thinking at all, making his mind blank.

He forced himself to go back. But just outside the door, as he saw light splashing from the room into the hallway, he stopped. Somehow, set against the darkness, the swath of yellow from the open doorway contained such a dreadful inference that he was overcome with breathless fear. It would be better if he could shout. But no sound would come.

Quickly he went back into the room, half expecting that it would now be empty, that it was an illusion projected from some dream memory or imagining. But now he accepted and looked for the first time with detailed attention.

Star Osborne was naked. A blood-stained sheet was drawn up only an inch above her knees. Dried blood, the color of shellac, ran down her thighs. In the area of the lower abdomen there was a great jagged wound from which blood had erupted. Here, the cruel dart with its winged barbs had knifed through the soft flesh and the wound had closed around the shaft of the harpoon. The long shaft angled upward from the body grotesquely—so deeply speared that she seemed impaled to the mattress. Her face was a bleached gray, her eyes stared at the ceiling and her mouth was open, lips drawn back slightly in a grimace. There was something odd about her features which at first Royce could not detect. They seemed larger, more accented than ever. He moved closer and then he understood. With a crude, uneven scissoring, her long hair had been cut off in a lopsided circle, almost to the crown of her head. This had the effect of extending and hardening her features. There was nothing of softness. She looked coarse and ugly.

Royce began to back slowly from the room. When wood frame touched against his thigh, he turned and went out the front door. In a daze, he left it open. He felt drained. His legs trembled.

Just below the steps he met Bruce Erickson approaching. Erickson came into the light that slashed from the living room out the open door. His lip, cheekbone and forehead were bandaged with strips of tape. The flesh

93

around one eye was puffed and purple. At first he looked at Royce dumbly. He peered into the apartment with its door ajar, back to Royce. Fear crept into his face, his mouth sagged.

"What's the matter?" he said. "Something wrong?"

Royce continued down the walk but Erickson grabbed his arm. "My God, what's happened!" His voice rose and cracked. "Where's Star?"

Royce looked at him, really didn't see him, wrenched away.

"Royce! You sick? Where you going?"

"To call the police," said Royce, his own voice sounding distant, detached.

There was a questioning silence behind him as he walked on. Then he heard Erickson scampering up the steps, heard him calling as from the mouth of a cave—shouting Star's name.

94

PART THREE

When Detective Lieutenant Moyer and Sergeant Wurdack were seated in Royce's apartment, Moyer said, "Now, Mr. Royce, would you first tell me your full name, your occupation and home address."

As he gave the information and Moyer took it down in a notebook, Royce studied the officer. He was a chunky man, not much above middle height, probably in his late forties. His dark red hair was sparse and combed straight back from a broad forehead. He had bushy brows, a prominent nose and sharp chin. The face was angular and, at first glance, appeared to be stern. But the Lieutenant's gray eyes and voice were mild and there was a hint of good humor about his mouth.

Sergeant Wurdack was several years younger and excessively tall, possibly six-three or -four. The contour of his heavy face was square, his features precise. In contrast to Moyer, who had deep furrows from nose to corners of mouth, Wurdack's face was unlined and deceptively bland of purpose. But his green eyes, Royce had noticed when they shook hands, were cool and watchful.

Shortly after Royce had phoned the police, a patrol car containing two uniformed officers had been sent from the Sheriff's Station in Malibu. The small station was not equipped for the intricate handling of homicides and after the officers had surveyed the situation, they had radioed the

Los Angeles County Sheriff's Department for investigators from the Homicide Detail. Meanwhile they had asked some preliminary questions and had kept watch to see no one entered Star Osborne's apartment.

While Royce waited outside with the patrolmen, Moyer and Wurdack had been busy within. And as they inspected the scene, a crime lab technician and fingerprint men from the identification section had arrived just in front of a deputy from the County Coroner's office. All of these were presently at work below. The stir of so many official cars converging on the building, the feeling of tense excitement which they had created, had sparked a small but steadily growing crowd to gather as close as the uniformed officers would allow them. To add to the confusion, reporters had come swarming in to jab everyone with their endless probing while photographers white-washed the night with flash pictures for the morning papers. The tenants had been told to wait in their apartments and this was the state of things as Royce was being questioned.

Lieutenant Moyer closed the notebook but held it in his hand. He was still for a moment. "Mr. Royce," he said, "have you ever been convicted of a felony?"

Royce looked at the officer with something of surprise and Moyer said, "No offense, sir. It's a routine question and generally we ask it of most everyone who might have some connection with a homicide."

"I have never been convicted or arrested for anything more than a traffic violation," he said.

"You discovered the body—correct?" said Moyer.

"Correct."

"And how did you come to do that?"

"Well, I hadn't seen Miss Osborne come out of her apartment all day and I wanted to speak to her. I knocked on the door and when she didn't answer, I went in."

"The door was open?" said Wurdack.

"Yes."

"Didn't you think that was strange?" said Moyer.

"At first I thought it was a little odd. But there had been a party at Miss Osborne's the night before with people coming and going and the door had been left un-locked. I think I was the last to leave and I certainly didn't lock it."

"When you left," said Wurdack, "where was Miss Osborne?"

"In bed. She was pretty tight and after we talked a

96

few minutes she fell asleep."

Wurdack raised his brows a fraction. "You were talking in her bedroom?"

"Yes. She wanted to lie down and I followed her. There was no choice with her. She did exactly as she pleased."

"I don't understand," said Moyer pleasantly. "There's always a choice."

"I mean," said Royce, "that if I wanted to talk to her, there was no choice. And I had to talk to her."

"Why?" said Moyer.

"She was causing trouble here and I could see it was getting out of hand. I wanted to persuade her to leave."

"What kind of trouble?" Moyer asked.

"She was creating jealousy among the men, passing herself from one to the other. And the women hated her. She had already caused a break between Rod Lindquist and his wife and a damn near fatal fight between Humphrey and Erickson. I thought that was just about enough."

"What about you?" said Moyer. "You had no personal complaint against her?"

"Not really. Only in the objective sense."

"You were never involved with her then?" said Wurdack. His tone was on the edge of sarcasm.

"In the beginning, yes. But not at the time she was killed."

"Murdered," said Wurdack with finality. "Butchered, I'd say. So when you left her, Royce, she was lying on the bed. Fully dressed?"

Wurdack made Royce uncomfortable. His tone, everything he said, was loaded with implication. But hell, they weren't investigating a bingo game. "No, she wasn't dressed," he answered. "She had a sheet over her, otherwise she was—naked."

Wurdack kept a stony face but glanced briefly at Moyer. Then he said, "I suppose she undressed right in front of you."

"Yes, as a matter of fact, she did. She wasn't the kind to think anything of it."

"After she was undressed," said Moyer evenly, "did you have sexual relations with her?"

"No," said Royce honestly.

"Oh, come on now," said Wurdack impatiently. "A beautiful doll like her. Of course you did." He stood, crossed the room, pivoted briskly. "Didn't you, Royce?"

97

Royce studied his shoes a moment, looked up, about to reply.

But then Moyer turned to Wurdack, said, "Harry, why don't you hop downstairs and see if Gillson or the print crew have come up with anything we can use." He got up quickly and looked out a window. "And have the local cops disperse that crowd. Blood-happy buggers'll mess up the whole area. Okay, Harry?"

"Yes, sir," said Wurdack. "Okay." He gave Royce an empty look and went out.

When the door closed, Moyer returned to his chair and said apologetically, "Wurdack's a fine officer but he's inclined to be a little blunt. We see a lot of crud in this game, you know."

"I understand," said Royce. "It all has to come out one way or another, I guess. If there's anything at all I can do to help . . ."

Moyer searched his pockets and came up with cigarettes, offered one to Royce and lighted it for him. He sighed, sat on the edge of his chair, leaning forward with the air of one who is about to exchange confidences. "There are a lot of personal details which may seem embarrassing and unnecessary to you, Mr. Royce. But in a case like this you never can tell what might have bearing."

"I know."

"Well, then—"

"Sure, she came up to my apartment and practically gave herself to me over a week ago. Naturally I didn't turn her down. But I didn't like her. In a way I was afraid to become too entangled with her. So after that I didn't have anything more to do with her. And anyway, she moved on to someone else the next day. Sooner or later she slept with every guy here, though I'm not sure about Lindquist. I mean, I don't know if it got that far because his wife was onto it."

Moyer nodded, smoke drifting from his nostrils. He had a mole on one cheek and he fingered it idly. "All right. So we've established that she was a pretty loose character, the Osborne woman. Of course she doesn't look too pretty lying down there now, so how would you describe this attraction that stood these guys on their ears?"

Ordinarily Royce would have given some pat answer.

98

But he perceived that Lieutenant Moyer was not without sensitivity. "Well," he said, "she wasn't really beautiful if you took her apart feature by feature and analyzed her. Of course, she was very well stacked, and yet that doesn't say it, either. It was more of a quality, Lieutenant. Only once or twice in my life have I met anyone remotely like her. She was so basically and startlingly sensual that she was like the thing itself—the undiluted distillation of sex. Almost a walking force of pure attraction. And in that way she was quicksand. And for that reason I suppose I didn't want to get too thick with her. She could own you and she knew it. It's intangible, but I don't know any other way to put it."

Moyer was intensely still and thoughtful. "I think I get you," he said, pulling a tobacco shard from his underlip. "I knew a girl once who . . . Anyhow, the Osborne woman was the sort a man wouldn't be able to leave alone after he got—what shall we say?—hypnotized by her?"

"Exactly," said Royce.

"You said she was making trouble, jealousy and all that. She slept around. She didn't make trouble on purpose but she was a nympho. Is that it?"

"Well," said Royce, "she may have been a nymphomaniac—incidentally. But she did make trouble on purpose. She went out of her way."

"Why?"

"I don't know. If I did, I might be able to give you the answer to the whole thing. It could have been a psychological quirk with her. And yet it seemed to me she was, I don't know, carrying out some plan."

"A plan? Now we're getting somewhere! What sort of plan?"

"Like she wanted to set people against each other. I'll go so far as to say she might have wanted some of these people here to kill each other."

"My God." Lieutenant Moyer stood, began to pace, paused. "That's pretty hard to swallow. But, all right. Let's say she wanted the tenants to strangle each other. All of the tenants? Can you narrow it down?"

"I could. But it would only be a guess."

"Go ahead and guess."

"Well, it appeared that she was trying to break up Humphrey and Erickson in particular. They were about as close as any two guys can get, I suppose. And it seemed like she wanted them to kill each other. They nearly did."

Moyer sat down again. "Humphrey and Erickson," he mused. He consulted his notebook. "They own this boat-building outfit, do they?"

"Yes."

"And this boat company is a moneymaker in a pretty big way?"

"I understand it is."

"Money," said Moyer. "The eternal motive. Might be something there. Now about the weapon, the harpoon. That was owned by Humphrey and Erickson?"

"Yes."

"And they were the only ones who had access to it?"

"No, I wouldn't say that. All the fishing gear including the harpoon was left in the boat under a tarp. But last night Erickson got sore at Humphrey and smashed the boat with an ax. The harpoon was probably right there in the open with the rest of the gear, in plain sight. Anyone could have taken it."

Moyer nodded, mashed his cigarette in an ashtray at his elbow. For a long moment he looked at Royce steadily. "Did you kill Star Osborne, Royce?"

Royce looked back at him just as steadily. "No," he said. "I didn't."

Moyer continued to study him, yet it was as if his thoughts had already moved on. "But you did sleep with her, so you must know something about her. What did she tell you about herself? What's her history?"

Royce shrugged. "She was strange about her past. She wouldn't talk about it very much. Except to say she came from Cleveland, her husband was dead and he had money."

"And that's all you know?"

"Well, I—"

"Come on, boy. C'mon! Which side are you playing? Don't fool around with me, boy."

Royce produced his wallet, removed the clipping and handed it over. Moyer studied it with growing perplexity. "Where did you get this?" he said.

"Let's say I happened to find it in her apartment. I used it to persuade her to leave."

"And was she going to?"

100

"She said she was. I threatened to show the clipping around."

"Why would she keep a damaging thing like this?"

"I don't know," said Royce. "She loved the limelight. Maybe she was secretly proud of her notoriety."

"This tells us something," said Moyer excitedly. "It looks like trouble—big trouble—was a habit with her. I think if we trace back far enough, we'll find a pattern. And maybe somewhere in that pattern, trouble was following her. And according to this clipping she was playing with another guy even while she was married. Her husband catches her in the act in a Cleveland hotel room. He beats the other guy unconscious, but then, if we can believe Star Osborne's testimony here, he thinks the rival is not just unconscious, but dead. So what does he do? He jumps out the window, eleven stories, leaving his poor widow thirty-six thousand dollars and knick-knacks. Now that's no J. P. Morgan estate, but it would buy a lot of cookies."

Moyer lit a fresh cigarette. "But here's a funny one. The husband, this Michael Osborne, goes up to the room all alone and walks right in, easy as can be. Did you ever hear of a pair like that jazzing it up with the door unlocked? Hell, no. So maybe she left it unlocked. And how did he know she was there in the first place? Unless she left a few clues around. Either she was a sadistic bitch or she had a scheme she was using over and over. I think we'll find she had a scheme."

"I think you're right," said Royce.

"But," said Moyer, "how does that scheme involve Humphrey or Erickson? Now maybe it doesn't. Maybe her past caught up with her and killed her. What do you think, Royce? You think an outsider crept in here, found that harpoon and killed her?"

"The way it looks, I would say no. But I remember that when I first saw her on the beach, she was watching the highway—the cars coming and going. She seemed very intent about it. But then it might have been some inward concentration. Because she was upset about something. She was cold as ice at first. And kept to herself. A couple of days later she changed completely, as if something had happened in the meantime."

101

"Well," said Moyer, "inside or out, it was a crime of passion. She had plenty of money in her purse. And in a felony-homicide the thief doesn't stop to cut off the victim's hair. You know, that part interests me. Not only did the killer slice the hair, but took it away with him—or her. If the hair was left, it would be a purely malicious act. But if a person clips hair from a body and takes it away, then it's almost an act of . . . reverence."

"Like an after-thought of regret," said Royce. "And worship."

"That's it."

"She really did have very beautiful hair," said Royce.

"Who of this bunch made special comment about it?" Moyer asked.

"Well—let me think. I don't—"

Wurdack opened the door and stormed in. "We got rid of the crowd," he said. "At least we got them so they're watching from the other side of the highway. My God, the news must have reached Santa Monica by now."

"How are the boys from ident doing?" asked Moyer.

"Prints all over the place. Some useless. Don't mean a thing. Big party the night before. They're still working, though."

"Did they get anything from the weapon, the harpoon?"

"A few smudges. No good. Jesus, the tip of that dart went clean through 'er. They'll have to cut the damn thing out. No problem with the shaft, detachable. Plop! and away it came. You could put your fist in the wound. Man, I tell you, if this was my first case, I'd be one green-faced cop. Even my hair would turn green."

"Well, c'mon then, Harry," said Moyer, rising. "We'll talk to the others." He turned to Royce. "Don't make any plans for a trip, Mr. Royce. We're going to need you again. And if for any reason you have to leave this area, please check with me first. Give me a call." He took a card from his wallet. "If you can't reach me at that number, ask for Sergeant Wurdack. But just stick around until you talk to one of us. And if you have any new information, call immediately."

"I'll do that," said Royce.

"Good night, sir."

"Good night."

Wurdack said nothing.

They went out.

two

Lieutenant Moyer and Sergeant Wurdack went down the stairs and stood for a moment by an open window of the apartment which held the body of Star Osborne. Inside, lights blazed, there was the sound of movement and voices. Two uniformed officers stood by the door, conversing in low tones. Two others guarded the walk at the entrance. At the curb and in the driveway, squad cars of the Malibu Sheriff's Station were drawn up, along with the official cars of the Deputy Coroner, the print and lab men, the two detectives from the Homicide Detail. Across the highway, knots of curious people gaped and made idle speculation, while others stood above them on a hill and peered down intently. Seeing the gathered police cars and the crowds of watchers, motorists swirling past braked to ask questions but were waved on by the officers in front of the building.

Lieutenant Moyer surveyed the scene, then stood for a moment puffing his cigarette and looking out to sea. "Well," said Wurdack beside him, "whatta you think?"

"About Royce?"

"Yeah."

"I like him. He seems a pretty straight joe. But a lot of guys I liked are in stir now. And some went to the little smoky chamber with the green door."

Wurdack inclined his head toward the Osborne apartment. "He was slipping it to her, all right, wasn't he?"

"Sure. So what? He wasn't lonely in that department. You think you would have shoved it away?"

Wurdack was silent. But then he said, "I think the bastard is covering something. I'd like to have some more digs at him."

"Don't worry, we haven't seen the last of him," said Moyer. He knew what was the matter with Wurdack. He had three kids, a big mortgage and a power-happy wife. He was bucking for more rank. Also, Wurdack had been a captain in the Army MP's and he couldn't forget that lowly sergeants used to salute him all over the place.

103

Even though he understood Wurdack, Moyer didn't particularly like him. Yet he had to admit that if you could take some of the edge off his tongue and some of the ramrod out of his back, you could hardly find a better cop.

"Listen, Harry," he said. "Go easy on these people. Don't baby them, but don't bludgeon them, either. Save it for the guy who shoved the spear. You can't open a tight clam with a crowbar, you know."

"Not unless you crack the shell," said Wurdack. "Anyway, it's your show. But I don't go for these characters who toss around a lot of pretty words to smoke up the crap they're hiding underneath."

Moyer sighed, produced a pocket flash and scanned his notebook. "Erickson is our next boy," he said. "He's supposed to be in the back. Let's have a look at him."

The little room by the car port was in complete darkness. Moyer hesitated at the door.

"Thought these birds were told to stay put," said Wurdack.

"We'll see," said Moyer. He knocked. When there was no answer, he knocked again and tried the door. It gave inward. "Leaving doors unlocked seems to be a habit around here," he muttered. He flashed his light, found the wall switch.

Erickson sat slumped in a chair. His head hung down and he stared vacantly at the rug. "Mr. Erickson?" said Moyer. "Bruce Erickson?"

Erickson did not look at them.

"Police," said Moyer. "My name is Moyer and this is Wurdack. Like to ask you a few questions, sir."

When Erickson sat as lifeless as before, Moyer, followed by Wurdack, moved closer for another try. "Son, I want you to pay attention for a minute and give me some information," said Moyer.

Erickson looked up slowly with empty eyes. He said nothing. His face was swollen lopsided, bruised and bandaged.

"C'mon, fella!" said Wurdack. "This is no taffy pull. Answer when you're spoken to. You can start by telling us who beat your face in."

Erickson spread his arms in a small hopeless gesture. "I loved her," he said tonelessly.

"Oh, Christ," said Wurdack.

104

Moyer waved him off, said, "Yes, I understand, boy, you loved her. But she was bad. She cheated on you. So you had to punish her, didn't you? She deserved to be punished and so you killed her. It was the only thing you could do. Isn't that it?"

"I loved her," Erickson repeated again, dumbly. His head went down.

"That's enough of that," said Wurdack. "Snap to and get on your feet. You can't talk with your head between your legs."

Erickson wasn't even listening. Moyer shook his head and took Wurdack aside. "He's in shock," he said. "We'll move on and get back to him later." Wurdack made a disparaging face and Moyer returned to Erickson's chair. "You've had a rough time, Bruce," he said. "But so has everyone else here. Now I'm going to give you another half-hour. Then I'll be back. See if you can pull yourself together. Because if you can't, son, I may have to take you in for questioning and I don't want to be forced to do that. Meanwhile, I want the lights on her, and I don't want you to leave for any reason. Is that clear?"

Erickson nodded without looking up.

Moyer and Wurdack strode out of the room.

"Now let's see if we have your story straight," said Lieutenant Moyer to Jay Humphrey. "You knew that Erickson was in love with Star Osborne. You thought she was a tramp and because he was your friend you didn't want him mixed up with her. So you decided that, by God, you were going to show him how easy she was and then he'd be so disgusted with her he'd break it off. On the spur of the moment you rigged up a little plot. During the party you passed Erickson the note and then you got her out on the beach bald naked where Erickson would catch you at it. And when you came back, you found the boat wrecked and Erickson waiting. That was when the fight started. Right?"

"Right," said Humphrey.

"But you were never jealous of Erickson. In fact, you had no use for the Osborne woman and so your personal feelings weren't hurt in the least when she took up with your friend."

Humphrey sat easy in his chair and spat a piece of ice back into his highball glass. He wore slacks and a white shirt rolled above the bulge of his biceps and open at the neck. There were small abrasions on the knuckles of the hand that held the glass, but otherwise, he looked to Moyer the picture of health. His tanned face was solemn but unemotional.

"I had about as much use for the Osborne dame as any other two-bit whore," he said.

"Sure," said Wurdack who stood tall with his hands clenched behind his back, while Moyer sat opposite Humphrey, "sure. And isn't it also true that you hated her! Because she had come between you and your friend Erickson. You hated her so much that you got your hands on the weapon you were so familiar with—your own harpoon that would pierce right through the tough hide and gut of a shark—and plunged it right about where this baby lived. The old trouble spot."

Humphrey showed the palm of his hand. "Now wait a minute, Sergeant. Just wait one minute before you jump to any conclusions. Maybe I did hate her—some. But hate means different things in different cases. It's a big word and it has as many degrees as a compass. Before I would risk my neck to kill anyone they'd have to upset my little world a lot more than Star Osborne, or the kid either."

Moyer sighed heavily. No matter how many of these investigations came and went, in the beginning, until the human debris was cleared and the routine set in, the bitter-sad stuff of life was a sour fermentation inside him. It never quite jelled and hardened into the cynical cement that walled away the ones like Wurdack.

"While you were intimate with Miss Osborne," said Moyer, "did she tell you anything about herself—her past?"

"Not one word," said Humphrey. "I couldn't reach her at all. And after a while I lost interest because it wasn't very important to me."

Somehow Humphrey's stoical calm, his glib answers, irritated Moyer. You met all kinds on homicide cases and yet the bland, nerveless or jaunty ones never ceased to amaze him. "Just as a point of interest to me, Mr. Humphrey," he said, "and quite off the record—why is it that you seem so completely undisturbed by the death of a person with whom you were intimate only a short time ago? Granted that you hated her—some—in your words. But still, don't you give any importance to human life? No one is all black and isn't everyone worth saving?"

106

For the first time Humphrey appeared to part with a little of his composure. He looked down, shifted in his chair, crossed and recrossed his legs. When he looked up again a small doubt had touched his features. "I have feelings, Lieutenant," he said. "I keep them covered."

"Is that all?"

"Well, she was no prize specimen. But she didn't deserve that kind of an end. She was vicious, but she was no shark. My God, I don't know . . . Anyway, what good does it do to cry now? She's dead. And we're all on the same road, not far behind her one way or the other."

Wurdack said, "All right. So if you didn't kill her, you've been around here long enough to have some idea who did. What about it?"

"To tell you the truth, I haven't had much time to think. It all happened so fast—"

"During the night," said Moyer, "did you hear any sounds, voices arguing, a commotion?"

"No, sir. I was rather loaded and I kicked off in a hurry."

Moyer consulted his notebook. "What kind of people are the Lindquists? Let's see, Rodney and Muriel Lindquist."

"Fine," said Humphrey. "Nothing against them, anyway. They just had a bad spat, you know. That dame had Muriel at Rod's throat. God, you should have seen—"

"Where will I find them?" interrupted Moyer.

"Up the stairs," said Humphrey. "Right overhead."

"Try to control yourself, please," said Sergeant Wurdack to Mrs. Lindquist who was in tears. "Just give us the facts. You can be sure no one will harm you while we're around. There's nothing to be afraid of, ma'am."

"Don't be an ass, Sergeant," said Mr. Lindquist. "You men aren't going to be here forever and of course there's a whole god-damn lot to be afraid of with some maniac running around loose. Can't you see you're upsetting her!"

"Just who do you think you're talking to, mister?" said Wurdack icily. "I don't care if you own the Golden Gate Bridge in San Francisco. You're here now. If you're not careful, you'll be answering questions under hot lights at the station."

"I'm sorry," said Lindquist. "Naturally, I'm on edge."

Wurdack grunted.

"We'll have a man on guard here tonight anyway, Mrs.

107

Lindquist," said Moyer. "And until this is cleared up, I'll see that a patrol car cruises by here night and day." It was almost a relief to see some emotion after Humphrey. And Moyer could understand why the poor woman was scared. In a way she reminded him of his daughter-in-law who was similarly plump and docile. Damned if he wouldn't have to have a talk with Wurdack. Though what had he done, really? After all, the husband was kind of sharp and acted like he was used to giving the orders. But obviously devoted to the wife.

Muriel Lindquist dried her tears and even smiled bravely. "It's just that now I know I must have been hearing it happen," she said. "Right at that very moment. And every time I think of it, I have to shudder. And I wonder if it couldn't happen again."

"We're being paid to see that it doesn't happen again, Mrs. Lindquist," Moyer said. "Now you say you heard something. Will you describe it exactly, please?"

Muriel Lindquist shifted in her chair to look at him more directly while her husband hovered over her, and Wurdack as usual stood squarely with his hands behind his back—like parade rest. Mrs. Lindquist had deep-set, kind-looking brown eyes. She certainly didn't do it, he thought. And then caught himself. Have to watch that. A cop knows anyone could do it.

"Well," said Mrs. Lindquist, "Rod—Mr. Lindquist—and I had a little quarrel and I couldn't sleep. So—"

"What sort of quarrel?" said Wurdack.

Muriel looked up at her husband and offered a wry smile. "It was about that woman, that poor girl, Star Osborne. I really despised her but now, well . . ." She twisted her handkerchief and sighed. "Last night at the party she was making a big play for Rod, for my husband, and he was keeping his distance. But later, after he had a few too many, she got him into the kitchen for some . . . some smooching. I don't blame him entirely. He's a man and vulnerable. But at the time it seemed like a minor tragedy to me and we had a fight."

"Naturally," said Moyer. "Go on with what you heard and how you happened to hear it."

"We left the party and we came up here. We argued for a while. At least I did. Because Rod kept saying he was sorry and he was too, well . . . soused—" she looked up and smiled at him again— "too soused to make sense

108

and we would talk about it in the morning. He was in bed first and he was snoring in a couple of minutes. I got undressed slowly. I was still thinking things over and still upset. Finally I put out the light and got in bed myself.

"I couldn't sleep. I lay there for quite a while and everything was quiet. Then I heard some pounding, kind of distant and muffled. I couldn't think what it was, but now I know it must have been Bruce Erickson smashing that boat. It was quiet again for a few minutes and then I heard voices and a shout. I thought it was the party running wild. After that—nothing. And I guess I fell asleep.

"I awoke again some time later with a splitting headache. I went into the bathroom and took some aspirin with a glass of water. I sat on the bed for a minute just holding my head. About that time I heard something faintly—a murmur of voices. I was groggy and it didn't register right away."

"You could hear nothing that was said?" asked Wurdack.

"No. And I wasn't listening attentively, anyway."

"Could you tell if it was a man or woman speaking—or both?" asked Moyer.

"Well, I certainly heard a woman. The voices had a kind of rhythm. You know, short bursts, like an argument. But they were withdrawn, held down the way people do when they're afraid they'll be overheard. As I said, it was just a murmur. But it does seem to me one voice was a shade deeper than the other. And then a voice that was definitely a woman's rose higher. It had an uncontrolled and frantic sound. It died suddenly, as if in the middle of a word. By that time I was really listening and trying to decide where the argument was coming from. There was a feeling of—I don't know—tension. And I was uneasy and beginning to be frightened. I knew the voices were coming from right nearby and I wanted to place them. I stepped to the door and opened it, listening.

"I heard two more words from a woman that sounded like, 'No, don't' or 'Oh, don't!' But I can't even be sure of that. It came from somewhere below. Then I heard something like a moan or a sob, low and drawn out. It was weird in the stillness—and terrifying. After that, it was absolutely frighteningly quiet. I stood there for about

109

another minute and then I tip-toed down to the walk in my bare feet and just a nightgown. I looked to see if there was a light from any of the apartments. But they were all dark. I went back upstairs and shook Rod.

"He was sleepy and gruff and he mumbled, 'What's the matter?' I told him what I had heard and he just said, 'God-damn party. Go back to bed, Muriel.' And then he was snoring again. So I thought, well, maybe it's just a silly little fight and someone did get slapped or punched, but it's none of my business. And anyway, if Rod wouldn't wake up, what could I do? So I went back to bed and eventually I feel asleep again."

"Before you fell asleep did you hear anything else?" Moyer asked.

"Nothing."

"Well, the other voice damn well must have been a man's," said Rod Lindquist. "Can you picture a woman wielding a harpoon, or even having enough strength to kill anyone with it?"

"I'll admit," said Moyer, "that I have to stretch my imagination to picture a woman thrusting that harpoon. But I can picture it just the same. A woman in a certain frame of mind, tormented and gone temporarily insane, and with the special kind of strength that comes from red-hot blind anger. Though actually, how much strength does it take to pierce the soft flesh of a woman with sharp metal? Yes, I can picture it, Mr. Lindquist."

"I wonder how come no one else heard any sounds?" said Wurdack.

"Did you ask Mr. Royce?" Muriel Lindquist said. "He's right over that apartment."

"No," said Moyer. "And that's a thought. I'll poke my head in there and then go on to Miss Bishop. Harry, to save time, why don't you finish up here."

"Right," said Wurdack.

"Lieutenant?" said Lindquist.

"Yes, sir?"

"We had planned to go on back home in the morning. Is that still possible?"

"I'd like to oblige you, sir. But I'm afraid not. Unless, of course, you can persuade someone to confess before morning. Good night to you both."

110

The hand with which Laura Bishop lifted the cigarette to her mouth trembled visibly. "And that's all I can tell you, Lieutenant," she finished. "From the minute she came out of that haughty pose of indifference to everyone, Miss Osborne seemed just bent on making trouble. Dear God, what an awful thing to happen to her. I don't know. I've given it a lot of thought. And it seems to me she was a type who was bent on her own destruction whether she knew it or not. She created these situations which she must have known would make people hate her. She just attracted violence."

Moyer became thoughtful. Laura Bishop looked rather prim sitting there with her hair swept back so severly, wearing the high-necked dress and scrubbed so clean that the flesh, taut against her cheekbones, fairly shone. A very nice, wholesome girl. Though a little too aggressively proper and . . . virtuous. The Lieutenant couldn't think of another word to suit her. Virtuous. Just the opposite of Star Osborne. For a moment the dreadful image of the harpoon impinged itself upon his consciousness. And he saw woman's virtue—an instrument of God—punishing at the very seat of evil.

"One thing more," he said. "From your story you appear to be the only one who was just an observer to this muddle that went on here. I mean, the others were either directly or indirectly and emotionally concerned with Miss Osborne. She didn't alienate you in any personal way?"

Laura Bishop blushed noticeably. "It's bound to come out sooner or later, I guess."

"Oh, yes," said Moyer solemnly. "Absolutely everything is bound to come out sooner or later."

"Well, I did have kind of a crush on Mr. Humphrey."

"Past tense?"

"Yes. The shock of this—this horrible murder and some things that Mr. Humphrey did prior to it, have

111

awakened me. He reminded me of someone that I . . . I loved long ago. I guess it was sort of wishful dreaming. Now I no longer have any feeling for him."

"But you did?"

"Yes."

"And you knew that he was one of Miss Osborne's lovers?"

"I was painfully aware of it."

Moyer smiled. "I appreciate your honesty. A final question and I won't take any more of your time. Mrs. Lindquist states that in the night or the early morning hours, she heard voices arguing and then a moan or sob. I just spoke with Mr. Royce and he said that he heard voices, too, though it sounded to him more like a cross between talking and whispering. He also thought he heard footsteps. He said he was never fully awake and it got mixed up with a dream somehow, and for that reason he didn't mention it to anyone. Now, did you hear anything at all?"

"I'm afraid not. I'm too far back here to have heard much unless it was very loud."

"I see." Moyer stood. "Well, if something else occurs to you, reach me at the number on the card I gave you. But unless we get a break I'll be around off and on for several days."

"I hope so, Lieutenant. Because I have the oddest feeling that it isn't going to end with Star Osborne."

The Lieutenant looked at her curiously. "It's a natural feeling after a thing like this," he said. "I wouldn't put too much stock in it. Good night, Miss Bishop."

As Moyer returned from a second visit with Erickson, he met Wurdack on the walk just outside. "Any luck with lover-boy?" said the Sergeant.

"He talked a little but he doesn't know much," answered Moyer. "He claims that after the fight with Humphrey he rode for miles down the highway. He doesn't know how far or how many hours he was gone. Then he came back and slept on the beach until eight-thirty or nine. He didn't hear or see anything. This morning he went to the owner—Macklin. He gave Macklin some tale about being in an accident and wanting to rent that little room so he could be quietly by himself until he felt better. Macklin gave him the key and he stayed there brooding. Then he decided to have a talk with the Osborne woman

112

and on his way he met Royce coming out of the apartment. From his attitude I got the impression that he has something against Royce. but he wouldn't admit to it. Anyway, the door was open and he went in and found the body. That's about it. He wouldn't talk about his relations with Osborne at all. The poor kid is about ready for the psycho ward."

"You could punch plenty of holes in that fairy tale," said Wurdack. "He has no alibi for his time."

"Sure," said Moyer. "And when you come right down to it, who has? You get anything more out of the Lindquists?"

"Nah. It strikes me that he's worried about her story and that's why he insists a woman couldn't have done it. He has something to worry about. She could have made that whole thing up."

"Of course," said Moyer. "But everything I know about this game tells me she didn't. I feel it. She rang true. She would have to be a damn fine actress with a damn good script to give an accounting in that detail and make it sound just right. Also, Royce heard somewhat the same thing, which seems to back her up. On the other hand, I don't rule her out for a minute. Or him, either."

"Yeah," said Wurdack. "He looks to me like a guy who might do anything if he got boiled up. Ah, hell, they all look bad to me. Except Humphrey, maybe. He's a cool one. I don't think he'd lose his head. So what next?"

"Next we get them all out here—fast," said Moyer. "And before they know what's happened, we make a search of every apartment."

"We don't have a warrant," said Wurdack.

"No, and we can't wait. So we ask for permission. If anyone refuses, well . . . we'll give that one some special consideration. But I don't think anyone's going to balk."

"What do we want to look for besides the usual things?"

"Some chopped hair," said Moyer. "Long hair, color of chestnuts. Now I'll take Royce and the Lindquists. You take the others. But get them out here so they won't be in the way."

"Right," said Wurdack. He looked toward the street. "Here comes the gut wagon," he said.

Moyer watched as the ambulance pulled to the curb

113

and two white-clad attendants leaped out and began to unload a stretcher. "They'll be taking her away in a few minutes," he said. "C'mon, let's get that search going."

four

Royce was standing about with the others just outside the Osborne apartment when George T. Macklin drove up. After a brief argument with the officers in front of the building, he got through and came hurrying up the walk. He was a tall fortyish man, slim with dark hair graying at the sides. He had a brush-cut mustache and was quite good looking—the sporty sophisticated type you could picture sipping Scotch and soda on the stern of a yacht between rounds of golf and sets of tennis. This impression was not entirely false. For while he hadn't been on the tennis courts or golf links in years, he was a big-game fisherman of note, owned two fine horses and was something of an expert at polo.

"What's going on here!" he said excitedly to the group in general. They all turned to look at him vacantly. No one answered.

Finally Royce took him aside and said, "One of your tenants—Miss Osborne—has been killed."

"Miss Osborne?" he said incredulously. "The widow? The beautiful one from Cleveland? I can't believe it! I got a call that there had been an accident or something here, but—"

"It was no accident," said Royce. "I think you'd better talk to Lieutenant Moyer from Homicide. He's up in my apartment but he'll be down any minute."

"From Homicide? No! Oh, Jesus. Oh, my God!"

Macklin's dark eyes widened with shock. Royce studied his rather pretty features with some awakening of interest. "Maybe you can clear up a little of the mystery about her," he said. "Everyone seems to have known her too well without really knowing her at all. Did she tell you anything about herself when she rented? Had you ever met her before?"

Macklin seemed nervously reflective. His eyes darted about and returned. "No," he said. "I never heard her name until she came into my office in the Palisades. She

114

was quite reserved. She was all business so I didn't press her. But she appeared to be a very high type."

"Yes," said Royce. "A very high type."

"Well, for God's sake, isn't anyone going to tell me what it's all about?" said Macklin. "How did it happen?"

Royce looked up to see Moyer coming down the steps. "That's the Lieutenant from Homicide," he said. "He'll give you the details, Mr. Macklin."

Macklin moved off and in a moment he and Moyer were in a huddle, with Moyer producing his notebook.

Not a minute later, when Royce had returned to stand with the others, the door opened and the white-clad attendants came down the three steps toting the stretcher covered with a tan blanket. They were followed by a man who must have been the Deputy Coroner for he carried the doctor's satchel and the professional's air of detachment.

The form under the blanket had just enough shape to identify itself as human while the imagination of the watchers lifted the covering and saw quite a different spectacle. The attendants were immaculate and empty-faced. To Royce the scene of the body's removal was twice as grim because it was all so antiseptic and impersonal.

The tenants were loosely clustered below the steps and as the body tilted down and came toward them, they backed away quickly and stood staring with various expressions of awe and revulsion. Occasionally they glanced into each other's solemn faces with a fearful kind of speculation, then back to the corpse being jogged away. All watched intently—except Erickson. The moment the stretcher had appeared in the doorway, he turned his back, covering his face with his hands.

The arrival of the ambulance had attracted still greater crowds and as the body was loaded the police had difficulty keeping them from rushing in for a closer view.

As the body was being lifted in place, Moyer offered a moment's distraction. With Wurdack, he stepped close to the tenants, said, "Everything appears in order and you may return to your apartments. Thank you for your cooperation. An officer will stand guard here for a day or two and a squad car will patrol the vicinity. While no one is under arrest, certainly you can understand that everyone is a suspect. Therefore, please don't stray far from this immediate area without checking with Sergeant Wur-

115

dack or myself. Any information which you may have for us will be handled with the strictest confidence. Thank you again."

The big door at the rear of the ambulance was closed and the attendants climbed into the cab. Lights flared and the vehicle eased away from the curb slowly, found its way into traffic and quietly faded, disappeared.

Without a word, the six broke up and went to their apartments. With the departure of the body, the crowd began to disperse reluctantly. Soon the print and lab men left, Moyer and Wurdack on their heels, followed by the reporters. The apartment below Royce which had held the remains of Star Osborne, was dark and empty. Looking from his window, Royce could dimly see an officer on duty outside the door. The officer lighted a cigarette and for a moment his cap and the hard lines of his jaw were visible in the flare. Then it was dark and still.

five

The story was displayed boldly in all the papers the following day. There were pictures—of the Pacific Tides, the tenants in a group, their faces stark in the white glare, the thrill-hungry crowds, and the body being carried down the walk. But not a single picture of Star Osborne as she was in life. None could be found. Bruce Erickson had two undeveloped and still in his camera. Somehow this information reached the ears of reporters. But neither persuasion nor threats nor sizable offers of cash could induce him to part with these pictures or even admit they existed. Meanwhile, though the news must certainly have reached Cleveland, the body lay in the morgue, unclaimed by a single relative or friend.

This was a mystery which was cause for much speculation in the papers. And because of the sensual atmosphere surrounding the crime and the sexual aspects implied in the manner of its commission, the scandal sheets enjoyed a sharp rise in circulation. But at the end of three days, when no solution was forthcoming, the story was consigned to the near oblivion of the back pages, replaced by the crash

116

of a commercial airliner, strikes, and political corruption.

Reporters came and went infrequently now, people seldom paused to gape at the building and on the fourth day, Moyer and Wurdack did not show at all. Finally the uniformed officer guarding the Osborne apartment was removed, though seemingly all of her belongings remained locked inside. A patrol car was still observed cruising the area, sometimes pausing in the night to flash a light over the building and the grounds. But even this event became rare. The tenants resented the apparent loss of interest and with less protection, their fears mounted. They began to complain and to request permission to leave. Complaints were soothed but permission to leave the county was denied. And further, the tenants were asked if they would cooperate by remaining at the Tides for "a short time longer."

There developed a certain attitude of resignation and slowly the group began to appear on the beach and to go through the motions of normal activity.

Stanley Royce was one who did not believe the police had lost interest. He knew they would never be allowed to become slack in the investigation of such a crime. And furthermore, he had seen on the face of Lieutenant Moyer the thoughtful patience of the dedicated officer. And about Wurdack there was a frighteningly relentless quality. No, surface indications were false. The Homicide detail would be hard at work and they would have assistance from other departments across the nation. However, his insight was not a great source of comfort to Royce.

What friendliness had existed among the tenants had all but vanished. The Lindquists remained mostly in the isolation of their togetherness. Erickson scrupulously avoided Humphrey, as did Laura Bishop, though when they did meet, she spoke to him with cool politeness. Humphrey himself seemed more and more withdrawn. The atmosphere was heavy and waiting.

Two small events that were exceptions to the listless routine occurred. Royce observed both from a distance. On the third day after the crime, Muriel came alone to lie on the beach. Almost immediately she was joined by Erickson. An hour later, Royce saw that they were still talking earnestly. Then Rod Lindquist dropped beside his wife and soon after, Erickson departed, a lonely figure slouching up the beach.

117

And on the following day, a thin, drawn-looking little woman with steel-rimmed glasses and a pinched expression of perpetual endurance, arrived in a battered Ford sedan. After much squinting and craning at the building, she found her way above to Laura Bishop's apartment and disappeared inside. Obviously, thought Royce, that is the mother.

He was returning from the little grocery store by the Malibu Inn when he almost collided with her as she hurried to her car. Her tight face was exploding with such anger that her skull threatened to burst from its skin. In passing, she impaled Royce with a venemous look, the unreasoning indictment of a stranger. Then she ducked her head, scurried to the tired jalopy and drove off with a clash of gears.

six

That same night, as Royce was perusing a manuscript with lapses of attention, there was a knock on his door. Laura Bishop stood before him. She was dressed in red toreador pants and a tight jersey which clung about the small firm hills of her breasts. She wore twice the usual make-up, carefully accented and piquantly applied so that her mouth seemed fuller, her eyes wide and bright. Once again her dark hair had been freed from the stern sweep and knot. It curved softly at her brow and fell long and loose to her shoulders. Her easy inviting stance, the expression on her face, were defiantly, aggressively female. She was a transformation.

Faintly, Royce was reminded of that faraway time when there was another knock on his door and Star Osborne stood in much the same manner. But Laura Bishop was cold sober.

"Well," he said. "This is a surprise."

"It's a surprise to me, too, Stan." Some small remnant of shyness remained in her smile. "The truth is that I'm suddenly and wretchedly lonely. And well, I couldn't think of anyone else I wanted to talk to. More than ever now, they're all such strangers. They even frighten me."

118

"Then I'll take that as a compliment," he said. "Why don't you come in?"

She looked beyond him into the soft light of the living room and there was a slight closing of her features.

"I see," said Royce, smiling. "Well—"

"No, you don't see, Stan. Not at all. It's just that I'd rather go for a little walk along the beach right now. All right?"

"Sure."

"I've been closeted in that stifling apartment so long now . . ."

"I'm convinced. Shall we go?"

She did not exactly steer him but she went in a certain direction and he just naturally followed. She moved casually and he was not aware of any purpose. They walked in the sand on the edge of the long grassy beach lot beyond the Tides.

"I wonder," she said, "why a big piece of property like this just lies here empty, going to waste?"

"All sorts of reasons," Royce answered. "The most likely one is that the owner is holding it for a big price."

Suddenly she halted and he found himself looking down into the gully, that small sheltered depression in the sand where he and Lindquist had come upon Star and Humphrey.

"It's no great decision," he said. "We go through it or around it—or we turn back."

She didn't answer but stood peering below with a peculiar fixity. Then she went down the slope and he followed. Legs spread, hands on hips, she gazed about her. "I think I'd like to stay here a while," she said in a small voice, as though she spoke to herself. She sank to the sand and with knees drawn up, lay on her back. Puzzled, he dropped beside her.

"You don't mind, do you, Stan?"

"I don't mind."

She was silent then and he looked up at the sky. There was a waning moon which blacked out altogether as a long bank of clouds began their drift across it. South, the ocean was an enormous black eye with a white lid at the shoreline. Obliquely across the eye, smoky light hung suspended above the twisting shadow of the coast. So steady and familiar was the rhythmic fall of waves that the ear discarded the sound—made it no-sound.

119

"I had thought," she murmured beside him, "that this place would at least have a morbid fascination for me. But, no. It has nothing any more. Just a place."

"What place? The Tides?"

"No. This place. Right where we lie."

And then frankly she told him about the contents of the note she had withheld from him and how she had seen Star and Humphrey naked in the moonlight.

"Of course Erickson saw it too," he said. "And that caused the fight."

"Yes."

"And you wanted to find out if you were really finished with Humphrey?"

"Yes. And I am. I feel nothing for him at all. Not even hatred. It wasn't his fault. I was dreaming an old dream over again and I invited just what I got. Oh, Stan, it's so good not to care, not to be driven. It might have gone on a ways but then when . . . when Star Osborne died I just woke up. It's a very peculiar thing. Freedom. And I got another kind of freedom today."

"Oh?"

"Yes. From my mother."

"That was she who went storming off in the Ford?"

"Uh-huh. The wrath of God departing in a 1947 Ford. Poor woman. She read it all in the paper and she came down here full of righteous indignation that I had allowed myself to become embroiled in this flesh-pot of sin and evil. Because, of course, there were some sly hints that maybe I wasn't just a pure little thing caught in an unavoidable mess. But how can you understand about my mother unless I tell you?"

She did.

"I was sitting there with her in the apartment this afternoon, listening to her tirade," she continued. "And then I wasn't listening at all, just looking at her and really seeing her for the first time. She grew in the wrong direction—down and down and down, smaller and smaller. Suddenly she seemed pathetic and ineffectual. She wasn't even my mother. Just a whiny little person chewed up by her own bitterness. And I wondered how she ever had a hold on me or got me to believe that stuff about men and carnal appetites. And the louder she got, the calmer I got. And when I could get a word in, I said, 'Mother, when this is over and I can leave here, I won't be home. I don't know

120

where I'm going but I'll send for my things. Maybe after a month or two we might get together and even be friends. But this living together with you holding the hand of God just over my head is finished—done.'

"Well, she went from hysterics to anger and back again. But when she saw it was all useless she flew out the door in a rage. And in my heart I said good-by to her. And right then I said the first real prayer I ever said in my life that I could believe—for her. And I was released. I was Laura Bishop, individual. And I knew I would never go back to stay."

"I like Laura Bishop, individual," he said. "I think she's going to be quite a gal."

"Oh, Stan, Stan, do you really?"

"Really." The sympathy he had felt for her was now replaced by a growing bond of closeness. And yet there was still a distance between them, an indefinable fear he couldn't shake.

"Don't misunderstand," she said. "But I feel as though you are the first man in my life. The first man worth calling a man and the first who doesn't fill me with some cringing dread. I want to kiss you, Stan."

"I'll be the last to object," he said.

She turned and melted against him. Her arms circled him and a soft hand came up behind his neck to hold him fast while her lips—the hungry lips of the long loveless—parted and searched and clung. It was not a kiss he would have expected from Laura Bishop—honestly and consumingly passionate. He forgot his fear and returned the kiss with a longing of his own. The kiss held and became a pulse of deep-soft desire.

"More, darling," she sobbed. "More, more, more! Make us both naked and take me right here in this spot. Don't ever, ever think I'm cheap, darling. But be my man and love me, love me. If I never make love to anyone else as long as I live, I won't be sorry it was you. But hurry, hurry!"

The desire remained but now he smothered it down. "Laura," he said. "Dear lost little Laura. You don't know what you're doing. Don't you see that whatever you may feel for me, you're just out to prove to yourself that you're a woman. You have this new freedom and you don't quite believe it and you want to grab it by the tail before it vanishes. Not only that, but you want to make love right

121

here in this spot. Why? To spit in the face of a ghost? And to convince yourself that Humphrey is once and for all meaningless? Damn it, I want you, Laura. But tomorrow when you saw your own motives you'd only hate yourself —and me, too. I'm far from noble. I'm just plain selfish. I don't want you to hate me in the morning. You *are* a woman, Laura. And you are free. You've already proved it. So save the rest for me when you're sure you mean it."

Through tears and anger, she said, "Oh, my God, my God! You sound almost like my mother. You make me feel ashamed all over again."

He caught her by the shoulders. "Now you listen to me, god-damn it! You think I don't want it even more than you do? I just paid you the biggest compliment that I . . ."

He lost the rest of it in his throat. The vague awareness of a presence had been nudging the back of his mind. But at that moment the presence had become a shadow which fell across them. And when he looked up the shadow was leaping back from the edge of the gully.

He jumped up and ran after the shadow. But the shadow was either swift or illusory. It was gone. He went back to her.

"Saw someone," he said. "Watching us. My God, it's a good thing we didn't . . ."

"Yes," she said. "It's a good thing we didn't." Her face was in darkness and if there was fear he couldn't see it. But smoldering rage lay deeply beneath the tone of her voice.

He tried to soothe her on the return but she wouldn't answer him. She opened her door and slipped behind it without a good night.

For a long time he couldn't sleep. He berated himself for being a dumb bastard with too much of the wrong wisdom. And too much heart and not enough animal grab. Grab it and the hell with it. Also he was beginning to feel something quite different for Laura Bishop. He was beginning to think she knew or could be tuaght The Language. His language. But now he wasn't sure. And he wasn't going to have a chance to find out.

So thinking, he sank beneath the first strata of sleep. And hovered there—neither awake nor deeply in slumber. Or at least so it seemed. For suddenly his eyes snapped wide and the fear was like the shock of knifing current, then like the breathless and loathesome certainty in the seconds before violent death.

The room was so dark it wasn't even a shadow. It was just a shapeless blotch poised above him. But it was real. It breathed in a rasping, agonized way.

They moved almost together. He was a split second earlier. The weapon came down with a merciless splat in the place where his groin might have been the instant before. He was off the bed and on the floor, rising quickly. The blotch was escaping from the room, ink sucked back into the bottle of the night.

He ran frantically even as he heard the front door closing sharply. He stumbled over furniture, fell, got to his feet. He found the door and got it open. In pajamas he took the stairs two at a time. But at the bottom, unless the blotch waited in hiding, there was nothing.

His eyes ran over the apartments and they were all dark. Then a light winked on. He placed it. Laura. Unmindful of his dress he was drawn toward it. Slowly he went down the walk and up the stairs. At the door he lifted his hand to knock. And then the light winked off again. He listened with his ear close to the wood paneling. He felt as if he could hear her breathing behind the door—rasping, strained. But, of course, he must be imagining it. He went away.

In his bedroom with the lights on he expected to find a ragged hole in the sheet, clean through to the mattress. But there was only the deep round mark where some heavy object had been swung down upon him. He might be dead. Or he might just be without his manhood. Either way . . .

There was no sleep for him that night. Nor did his lights go out until morning.

seven

Lieutenant Moyer came on the wire at last. "Moyer," he said wearily.

"This is Royce out at Pacific Tides, Lieutenant. I tried all morning to get you or Sergeant Wurdack. No luck."

"Yes, sir. Well, we're in and out a lot, you know. Something I can do?"

123

"Someone tried to make a second corpse out of me last night." Royce related the incident without mention of Laura Bishop. "I can't understand why anyone would want to kill me in particular," he closed.

"We'll have to give that some thought," Moyer said with an infuriating lack of concern. "No idea who it was?"

"None. And, Lieutenant . . ."

"Yes?"

"This is a mighty dangerous place to be living right now."

"I agree. But keep your head and don't spread the alarm. We don't want a panic out there. Now, how did this bird get in if your door was locked?"

"It's embarrassingly simple, Lieutenant. There's a window at the head of the stairs. It opens on to my living room. He poked a little hole in the screen and the rest was easy."

"It's better to breathe a little stale air than none at all, Mr. Royce. Keep all windows that can be reached closed and locked. Meanwhile we'll tighten up the patrol around there."

"Thanks. But that news isn't exactly a sleeping pill. Are you making any progress, Lieutenant?"

There was a pause. And a sigh. "It's slow," he said. "But we know what we're doing or we wouldn't be here. Thanks for calling, Mr. Royce. If the least thing unusual occurs, get in touch."

"I hope I'm able to next time. So long, Lieutenant."

" 'Bye, sir."

Coming out of the phone booth he met Laura Bishop. She was in her bathing suit and walking toward the beach. She paused, gave him a queer litle smile. He waited. Her eyes were shy and roving before they returned to his face.

"I'm sorry about last night," she said. "And you were right. It was a very bad idea. In a way, I guess I was trying to prove I had really cut myself off from Mother. But don't think you were just an experiment, Stan. It couldn't have happened with anyone else."

She looked so guileless and he wanted to like her without reservation. "Well," he said, "maybe it's just ego talking, but I'm rather inclined to believe that."

"Then we're friends? And you're not mad at me?"

"If I was anything at you, it wouldn't be just mad." He was thinking again of last night and a single light that winked on and off. "Did you sleep well?" he asked.

124

"Not very, I'm afraid."

"When you can't sleep, Laura, what do you do? Just lie there in the dark, read, go for a walk?"

"Walk? Alone? Not around here. Mostly I just lie in the dark and think."

"Well now, I walk. Sometimes. Like last night." He watched her closely. "I looked up at your apartment and for a minute I was tempted to knock on your door. Because I saw you had a light on. But then the light went out."

Her lips formed a circle of surprise. Her eyes were guarded. "A light? Unless I was walking in my sleep . . ."

"Unless I see things like shadows—and lights." And if he really did see the shadow while Laura was with him, then wouldn't she be entirely innocent?

Her lips broadened into a smile. "I remember now. You know my living room is also my bedroom. And if I get up to go to the bathroom, I put on a light for a moment to find my way." She chuckled. "I'm the type who is completely night-blind. Even in a movie, unless someone takes my arm, I stumble all over myself."

"That solves it," he said with a conviction he didn't quite feel.

"Well," she said, "why don't you go put on your trunks and join me on the beach. We might even go for a swim. For some reason I feel almost normal today."

He hesitated. "All right, then. In about five minutes."

Night came and there was dinner with Laura at a small café almost next door. Humphrey was there, too. Alone. He waved but made no attempt to join them. Then there were drinks in Laura's apartment—a rather gay time in which there was talk about everything but murder and complex. No love-making. His suspicion of her faded and she was restored to him whole. She was sensitive, warm and intelligent. She knew part of The Language. He would teach her the rest. He kissed her once, at the door.

It was five minutes before ten and he was back in his apartment. It was another hot night for Southern California, but in spite of this, he locked all the windows but those in his bedroom. To reach him there, someone would have to climb straight up a wall. Or use a ladder . . .

Fully dressed, he lay on his bed, reading. His thoughts

125

wandered. His eyes ached. He put out the light. He remained on his back, propped with a pillow. He thought of nothing now. He allowed his eyes to grow accustomed to the dark until he could identify objects in the room. He found that he was tense and rigid. He shifted his position. That was better. But now he was listening. Cars on the highway. The snort and drone of those big trailer trucks ploughing the night, making furrows of light. And in the empty spaces the somnolent cadence of the ocean. Nothing more.

Faces swam over the screen of his mind: Rod and Muriel Lindquist. Humphrey and Erickson. Laura Bishop. Mrs. Bishop. How unspeakably angry she was in that moment when their eyes met. The wrath of God . . . And then the face of Star Osborne. The dead face. He could see it no other way. Dead—with the hair chopped. And the big mouth of the wound closing around the shaft. And the animal thing which walked inside her loosed from its confinement, prowling ethereal woods, looking for another mortal cave to befoul.

The pictures slid backward and stopped at Erickson. Where was he? He hadn't appeared all day. Was he closed in that little room with his secret torment? How long could you stay folded in a box with the fetid melancholy of your own naked thoughts?

Thinking was an agony of doubt—useless. Reading also. And sleep was a shuddering impossibility. He got up and paced the living room slowly, his eyes acquainted with the dark. He opened the door and stood outside a moment, drinking air. A night of hovering clouds and the close dankness that hints of rain, the eyes of the building lidded in sleep.

He turned to go in when from somewhere below there came the thin scratch of metal—a veiled, tiny sound. He stood rooted, frantically thumbing through his memory for a sound like it. Then it came again with an accompanying snap, and he knew. A key. Key in lock.

He peered over the stairrail in time to see the door to Star Osborne's apartment swing slowly to until it met the jamb but didn't lock.

Now he thought about weapons. A knife? A club? Or the element of surprise and the coil of muscle. Because of the time factor, he chose the latter and sneaked down

126

the stairs on balls of feet, glad that this time he was dressed.

Silently he eased the door closed behind him. He crept over the living-room floor, testing each step for a give-away creak of warped wood beneath rug. He was guided by the stealthy sounds and the feeble dance of light from the open door of that infamous bedroom. He had not been in the apartment since that time when he looked down upon the grotesque horror of her mutilation. And though she was gone, the smell and feel of death seemed to fall from the deepest darkness, particles of decay settling upon him, smothering him.

He was in the little hall now and faintly heard a hollow, metallic rattle. Then he stood in the doorway and saw the crouched form of a man across the bedroom. The man knelt beside a gas panel heater from which he had removed the square of grille enclosing the pilot. He held a large chrome-plated flashlight in one hand and a small metal box in the other.

The man's face was turned away. Now he opened the box and inspected the contents. He removed an envelope and from the envelope a letter. He merely glanced at the letter and returned it immediately. He closed the box and set it on the floor with the flash. Quietly he began to replace the grille. As he did this, Royce, who had been sneaking forward, stood just behind him.

As the man set the grille in place, his hands lingered for a moment incongruously. The warning stole upon Royce at the same instant the man whirled and pulled his legs out from under him. Royce fell. But before going down he was already making himself loose and pliable, ready to spring. He recoiled and shoved to his feet. With flash and box, the man was hurling himself through the doorway when Royce caught his coat. And then his neck in the lock of his arm.

In the seconds before the flashlight whirled and came down on his head in a shower of light, Royce saw who it was. The man getting away as Royce sagged and tried to keep from going down was George T. Macklin.

Minutes later, with only the ache and fuzziness of a bad hangover, together with a small lump on his head, Royce was in the phone booth, calling Moyer. The flat voice told him the Lieutenant wasn't in, nor was Wurdack. They were out on assignment and couldn't be reached. Royce thought of calling the Sheriff's Station at Malibu. But Macklin would be long gone.

And God only knew in what direction.

eight

      Across the highway and up on the hill overlooking the Pacific Tides there were other apartment houses and also private dwellings. All of these were dark now. The structure directly opposite and above the Tides was a small house, rental property which had just been completed but not yet leased. The living room had sliding glass doors which opened upon a patio and provided a fine panorama of the entire coast.

Presently these doors were swung wide and Lieutenant Moyer sat just outside them peering through extremely high-powered binoculars specially suited to night work. These glasses were so immense that they had to be sustained by a tripod. Sergeant Wurdack was at Moyer's elbow, speaking quietly into the mouthpiece of a walky-talky, a pint-sized radiophone. Now he passed the instrument to Moyer, saying, "It's Nate Sarno on the horn, Lieutenant. He's back in the lot again, bellied down in the grass about a hundred yards east of the Tides. Wants to report on Macklin."

Moyer pressed the receiver close to his head. "Yeah, Nate," he said. "Everything under control?"

"Ten-four," replied the officer. The voice was clear but had a slightly mechanical sound. "Thirty-one has our friend ten-fifteen. Keegan on the way with the box. Any minute now. Get a load of contents! Too hot to hold in your bare hands."

"Okay, Nate. Good work. Is that all there was in the box? That one item?"

"No, sir. But I didn't have time to give it a good look. You want thirty-one to run in with the suspect?"

"Wait until I check the box," said Moyer. "Will call in a few minutes. Ten-four?"

"Ten-four."

128

Moyer gave the receiver to Wurdack, said, "Nate says Keegan's on the way up with the box. Chambers and Parnell have Macklin in custody down the road in the car. They wanted to take him to the station but I said hold off until we get a peek at the box."

Wurdack grunted and Moyer resumed his surveillance, sighting the binoculars on the Tides, then scanning left across the empty lot, returning all the way to the other side of the building. "I guess Royce went back to bed," he said. "I lost him in all the excitement."

"Lucky the moon finally gave us a smile through the god-damn clouds," said Wurdack. "Or you wouldn't be able to make out one guy from another."

"True," said Moyer. "But give me just a little light and I can read fine print with this baby."

At that moment Keegan walked in through the back way and handed him the box. "Okay, thanks," said Moyer. "Go down and stay on post near Sarno until we decide if we're ready to wrap it up."

As Keegan departed, Moyer and Wurdack stepped into a back room, gave it light, spent several minutes with the box and returned. Wurdack got hold of Sarno and passed the receiver to Moyer who said, "I don't think we'll fold yet, Nate. The way this junk reads, I have a hunch we're not finished. Keep observing the ten-twenty until further notice. Thirty-one can take the suspect in and then hop back. Evidently he's just going to sing that one song and there's nothing else here on him. So hold position and keep those glasses peeled. Ten-four?"

"Ten-four."

"How about that letter, Lieutenant," said Wurdack. "You ever read worse filth?"

"Nope. Except on bathroom walls. His language is a little better. Means the same thing, though."

"What did Nate say was Macklin's line? How did he know where to find the box?"

"You want the whole story, I'll give it to you in a nut," said Moyer. "Macklin got cozy with Osborne when she came back the second time to plead for a front apartment. He flipped her on his yacht. He was burning a hot torch for her and wanted to keep the show going. But she said no dice, said he could write and then maybe they'd get together when she was ready to leave. Something funny there. I think she was setting him up in case some other

129

patsy flunked out. After he did write her he got panicky about the letter lying around where it might be seen. He called her and she said she'd hide it, but it was too good to burn. Hah! He told her the best place to keep it was the gas heater in the bedroom. It wasn't working and who'd ever look there? We sure didn't because our main interest was in searching the live ones. Anyway she must have agreed because that's where he found it. End of tale. Except that we know Macklin is a lecher and was once convicted of attempted rape. Got off with a suspended sentence. If it wasn't for the other stuff in this box, I'd say he's our boy. But now I'm not so sure. The one thing I've been really hoping would happen all these nights, hasn't. Everything else but. So now we'll see."

"I'll bet that's not half the scoop," said Wurdack. "It's got to be Macklin. Guys like him repeat and sooner or later they fall off a limb. Why do we waste time here? Let's go to work on the bastard."

Moyer shook his head. "Don't forget the other letters in the box. I think it's going to swing just the way we thought after we dug into her background. My God, what a con girl! Nope, we wait another hour. And then if we don't pin it on Macklin, we come back again tomorrow. Someone's liable to get jumpy and make a run for it. That's why I yanked the guard in the first place."

Wurdack sighed and sank into a chair. "All right," he said. "I didn't have plans. Except for sleep."

One hour and seven minutes later, as Moyer was giving Detective Nate Sarno instructions to withdraw, Sarno went dead in the middle of a sentence. "Hold it, Lieutenant," he said. "I think I see someone coming. Yup! Take a look. Moving around the southeast side of the building. Heading northeast across the lot, right toward me!"

Moyer held the radiophone in one hand, slowly scanning with the binoculars. "Got it, Nate! But I don't make yet."

"Neither do I. But coming closer. There! Right in focus. But this one I don't know. Ducked by to the left. Should be close enough for you to make now with that big job."

"Just wait," Moyer said. He placed the radiophone in his lap and gave full concentration to the figure below, adjusting focus. "Now!" he said. "Well, I'll be damned. And burying something or digging it up. This is it! Take

130

a look, Wurdack." He bent out of the way.

Wurdack kneeled down and squinted into the lenses. "I'll be a son-of-a-bitch!" he said finally. "You guessed wrong, Lieutenant. This one is a surprise."

But Moyer was busy on the radiophone. Sarno was saying, "Shall we close in and arrest?"

"No!" said Moyer sharply. "Repeat. Ten-thirty-four. Do not arrest. Mark that spot and observe suspect. But do not arrest. Clear?"

"Ten-four."

"I'm going down," said Moyer. "Come on, Wurdack."

nine

Royce hadn't even tried to sleep. Still dressed, he sat for a long time in the dark of his living room, figuring what to do. One thing was certain, it was practically over now. When he told his story they'd find Macklin and that should end it. Tomorrow, or at least the next day, he'd be able to leave. My God, but that would be a relief. The whole thing had reached out and come so close to him it almost cut him down. Yes, in a couple of nights he would be able to sleep again. Maybe. If he could ever forget. If he could ever stop looking over his shoulder on dark nights and being just a little afraid.

But there were still things to be done. If he only knew where Moyer and Wurdack were. After a timeless time of pondering he got up and went out. He looked carefully around the building. All was dark, all quiet. His thoughts a jumble of indecision, he began to walk, only half aware of direction.

In ten minutes he was back again. He stood on the stone patio, stood dumbly staring at the vacant-eyed building. The feeling that he was being stared back at came over him slowly, but with overpowering conviction. He should not be so afraid now, but nevertheless he was almost trembling with strain. He began to search the windows—up, down, over, up, down . . . And then he caught the smallest movement far to the left. He shut his eyes, opened them and turned his gaze toward the high-

131

way side of the building. Up, down . . . Down!

There was someone standing completely motionless in the doorway to Erickson's cubby hole. Erickson? It looked like him. About the same stature. He didn't know whether to advance or remain standing. Whether to speak or not to speak. He wanted to shout.

He looked away as though he had seen nothing, but walked casually in the direction of that doorway, on down the walk so that he would go right by. Then he would turn and light a cigarette. And while he was lighting it, he would take a good look.

Passing the doorway he saw from the corner of his eye that the door was open but there was no one there. He took half a dozen more steps. From behind, bulging arms like sinuous steel encircled him and held him in a strait-jacket. He writhed and kicked but it was useless. And now a forearm forced his chin up and sank deep into his neck. He sobbed for air. A hand grabbed him by the hair and pulled his head back. And then he was released.

"Royce, god-damn it, it's you!"

He turned. He looked. It was Humphrey. "What the hell's the idea?" Royce said. "I ought to club you good!"

"I didn't recognize you," said Humphrey, unperturbed. "Where were you just now?"

"For a walk," said Royce. "If it's any of your business. I couldn't sleep so I hiked up to the Pier."

"If you went to the Pier," said Humphrey, "how is it you were coming from the other direction when I saw you?"

"I went past the building and turned back," said Royce. "Have they elected you sheriff?"

Humphrey shifted in position. "Seen Erickson?" he said.

"Not today. Or tonight, either. Why?"

"I don't know what happened to him. I was waiting for him. Went out and left his door open. He doesn't come back he'll be in trouble with the cops."

Royce didn't answer. He was still unnerved and also angry. He would like to tell Humphrey what had happened, had to tell someone. But damned if Humphrey would be the one. "Next time be careful, Humphrey," he said. "You could get killed jumping people in the dark."

A light went on above and Muriel leaned out the

132

window. "What's the trouble?" she said. "Who are you down there?"

"Royce and Humphrey," said Royce. "No trouble. Not now anyway. Lots of excitement earlier."

"What excitement?" said Muriel nervously.

Royce made a decision. "I'd like to talk to you and Rod about it," he said. "May I come up?"

Muriel hesitated. "All right," she said. "Come ahead, if you don't mind the way we're dressed. I'll get Rod up and we'll make you a drink. You, too, Jay."

"No thanks," said Humphrey. He turned to Royce. "What's going on?"

"Tell you later," said Royce, and went up the stairs.

Muriel was a long time coming to the door. Yawning, looking bulbous in a pink negligee, she ushered him into the living room. Pale and groggy, Rod was coming out of the bedroom, smoothing back his hair. He wore pajamas, a monogrammed burgundy robe and slippers. "Come in and sit down, Stan," he said. "Muriel says there's been some trouble. What now? Drink?"

"Thanks. Bourbon. On the rocks."

Rod made himself busy in the kitchen. Muriel composed herself on the sofa, smiling her shy smile, listening as Royce told about Humphrey, saving the Macklin part until Rod came back with a tray of drinks.

"Well," said Rod, drink in one hand, cigarette in the other, "let's have it." He seemed only mildly concerned, had the slightly sardonic look of someone who is about to hear a ghost story. But as Royce launched into the incident, his eyes narrowed with interest.

Royce was completing the account when there was a strenuous knock on the door. Rod and Muriel looked at each other. Rod opened the door.

Lieutenant Moyer glanced at Rod fleetingly and without comment. From his position near the door, Royce could see that the Lieutenant's eyes were stern and exceedingly alert. They looked past Lindquist over his shoulder at Royce himself. Royce could feel the uneasiness beginning to crowd him.

Moyer stepped in without being invited. He was dogged by Wurdack whose square features were inscrutable. Rod Lindquist closed the door slowly, his head cocked as though straining for some foreign sound. Muriel frowned. No one spoke. It was a pantomime which Royce saw with an underwater quality of both magnification and distortion.

Wurdack leaned back against the door, chewing on a toothpick. His coat was open and the holster and butt of his service revolver were visible. Moyer carried a small green metal box and a folded newspaper. The box looked familiar to Royce but it was inconceivable that it could be the same one. And yet . . .

Moyer paused before Royce's chair, turned to Muriel and Rod Lindquist. "If you don't mind," he said, "we would like to talk with Mr. Royce."

"Go right ahead, Lieutenant," said Rod. "Perhaps we should leave."

Moyer was pulling up a chair close to Royce and seemed not to hear. He sat down heavily, placed the box and newspaper in his lap. He built a pyramid with his hands and studied the achievement absently. Silence grew interminably upon the room. Wurdack's jaw barely moved around the toothpick.

Royce studied Moyer's sad thoughtful face and groped for words to fill the void. "As a matter of fact," he said, "I've been trying to reach you, Lieutenant. It's about Macklin. You see, I . . ."

Moyer nodded. "We have Macklin in custody," he said.

"How could you?" said Royce with astonishment.

Wurdack removed the toothpick. "We picked up Erickson, too," he said.

"Erickson?" said Royce.

"Emotionally," said Moyer, "Erickson is a child. He was hurt and he had to hurt back. To a certain extent, his account of his time the night of the party was a lie. He drove off in a stew but he returned in half an hour. He couldn't do without Star Osborne, so he was going to forgive her. The lights were on in her apartment and he walked in. The bedroom door was closed. He listened and he heard your voice. Even for him that was too much in one night. He damn near killed himself burning rubber down the highway again."

Moyer paused, dropped his head to the back of the chair and addressed the ceiling. "When Erickson found out she was murdered, he figured you did it, Royce. You were the last one with her, and Mrs. Lindquist told him Osborne had slept at your place soon after she arrived here. So he broke into your apartment in the middle of the night. He was carrying a club. He didn't know exactly what he was

134

going to do, except force you to confess. Then when you woke up suddenly, he swung at your legs—a reflex action."

"You believe that?" said Royce.

"I'm inclined to," said Moyer. "He could have killed you, but instead he ran. And I have a certain sympathy for the boy. He's unstable, confused. Of course, if you want to press charges, we could hold him for trial. Otherwise, I'm going to release him in the morning."

"If he didn't do it, I don't want to crucify him," said Royce. "As far as I'm concerned, let him go."

"Very generous of you," said Moyer pleasantly. "I guess that's about all then." He began to lift himself from the chair, sank back again. "Just one more thing. I'm a very curious guy." He swung his head around abruptly. "At twenty minutes past one this morning, what were you doing out on that empty lot next door—Mrs. Lindquist?"

Muriel recoiled as if she had been struck in the face. Then she craned her head forward as though she had heard some obscenity. "Me!"

"Oh, come off it!" snapped Wurdack. "We were across the way, watching you through glasses the whole time." His words had a shocking effect. Everyone seemed to have forgotten he was there.

Muriel looked down and twisted an edge of her negligee. "I was just walking," she said in a thin tired voice. "I couldn't sleep."

"Crap!" said Wurdack.

Moyer simply looked at her steadily, fingering the mole on his cheek. Then slowly he unfolded the newspaper on his lap. Inside was something bunched, pale-blue and rubbery. It was fashioned like a pouch, the ends tied together with a piece of string.

"This," said Moyer, "would be a section of shower curtain from your bathroom, Mrs. Lindquist. I noticed it was missing when I searched the place." He untied the string and opened the improvised pouch. "And this," he said, "would be human hair, color of chestnuts, wouldn't you say?"

He held up the long curling strands, jaggedly cut and held together with a rubber band. Even now, under the light, there was a glint and shine to them.

"Oh, my God, my God," groaned Rod Lindquist.

"We picked this up where you buried it in the lot," said Moyer, still holding the hair aloft.

135

Muriel stared at the hair, fascinated. She began to nod and nod and nod in a terrible rhythm. "Yes," she said, "I did it. God help me, I did it."

"Muriel!" said Rod. "Are you insane? Of course you didn't do it! I don't know where you got the hair, but you didn't do it. Tell them the truth!"

Muriel didn't look at him but continued to stare at the strands which Moyer had dropped back upon the unfolded fragment of shower curtain. "She was the most evil woman I've ever known," she said in a hushed voice with a hypnotic cadence. "If there was any good in her, I never saw it. She used and soiled every man she touched. I couldn't let her do that to Rod. And I couldn't lose him." She looked up at Moyer. "But that isn't why I killed her. It was self-defense."

"Huh!" snorted Wurdack.

"Tell us why you think it was self-defense," said Moyer in a soft voice.

"That night," said Muriel, sounding strangely calm now, "she finally got Rod so I could see he was going to give in to her. She was going to have him like all the rest. And I became obsessed with the idea that I was going to lose him. So, long after the party, while Rod was asleep and after I saw Mr. Royce go out her door, I got dressed and went down there. I had nothing in mind except that somehow I was going to get her to leave—threaten her, offer her money, anything. There was one light on in the living room and the door was unlocked. I went to her bedroom and opened the door. It was dark. I put on a light. She lay on her side—naked, except for a sheet drawn up about halfway. She was asleep.

"That harpoon thing was standing in a corner of the room next to her bed. I don't know why. It seemed odd. I thought maybe she had it there for protection. She had every reason to be frightened. I went over and touched her. Then I shook her. She had been drinking heavily and she wouldn't wake up. I didn't know what to do. I just stood looking down at her. Her long hair flowed back over the pillow. I couldn't take my eyes off it. It was beautiful, the only really beautiful thing about her. And I hated it.

"Not long before, in a crazy unhappy mood, I had my own hair cut short. It was an awful mistake. I was already getting fat and it made my face look ugly and bloated. When Rod saw it he could hardly keep the revulsion from

136

his eyes. And . . . and so while I was standing there, I thought how unattractive Star Osborne would look without her long hair. I remembered seeing a pair of scissors on the dresser. I went over and picked them up. They were pointed and sharp. I stood over her and for a moment I could hardly control the urge to sink them into her. But I . . . I didn't have the nerve. So I grabbed the loose ends of her hair in my hand and snipped high on her head.

"After the hair was cut, it lay there detached on her pillow. I was going to leave it but I got the idea that maybe a clever hair stylist could fix it to a band or make a partial wig out of it. So I scooped it up and went out to the kitchen. I found a paper bag and dropped it in. Then I went back to the bedroom to put out the light.

"She was standing there nude before the mirror, fingering her hair with the most amazed expression. She turned and saw me and she said, *"You* did this. *You.*" She began to curse me. It was like a snake hissing. And . . . and I was so shocked that she had awakened, I was unable to move or speak.

"She began to back away from me toward the wall. And suddenly she had that harpoon in her hand. She came toward me with it and when the point was just a foot from my chest, I found my senses. I grabbed it and twisted. We struggled. She fell back against the bed, toppled onto it, still holding the point toward me and pushing. I went out of my mind with fear. With all my strength I turned the thing around and plunged it into her stomach. I didn't realize what I had done until she moaned and gasped and slowly fell back dead.

"I snatched the bag with the hair, put out the light and ran out. When I got up here, I hid the bag under some things in a drawer, got quietly undressed and into bed without waking Rod. When the police came, I was insane with fear and I sliced off a piece of shower curtain, wrapped the hair in it and concealed it under my clothing. Then . . . then tonight was the first time I felt it was safe to bury it . . ."

Muriel began to weep softly.

"She had a long time to think that one up," said Wurdack to Moyer. "Can you imagine a jury believing it was self-defense. Two babes struggling over a harpoon, no witnesses. Jury would be out about twenty minutes. Bang!—guilty—first degree. Gas hell out of her, says the judge."

137

Moyer stood, crossed the room, turned and leaned against a wall. "I don't know," he said. "She might get life."

Muriel sobbed.

"The thing that is almost impossible to believe," continued Moyer, "is that she would carry that hair around all this time and then bury it, when she could have cut it up and flushed it down the toilet. Why, Muriel?"

She shook her head. "I don't know myself," she said through tears. "I couldn't seem to think sensibly at all."

"If it was self-defense," said Wurdack sneeringly, "you would have reported it to the police in the first place. Then you might have had a chance. But not now, lady. Even a rookie lawyer would tear you apart in court."

"Well," said Moyer, "that's not our problem. Our work is done. Get dressed, Muriel, and come with us."

Royce watched unbelieving as Muriel got slowly to her feet. It must be a grim joke, while all along Macklin had done it. Not Muriel. Let it be Macklin! Poor fat pathetic Muriel.

Royce looked at Rod Lindquist. His face was gray and beads of sweat stood on his forehead. Through it all he had acted as if he was being told Muriel was dead in some dreadful accident and he refused to believe or understand.

Now as Muriel stood, he came beside her and laid a soft hand on her shoulder. She reached back and squeezed the hand, smiled bravely into his face. At that moment, Rod turned to Moyer.

"I'll admit," he said in an oddly constricted voice, "that for a while she had me convinced that her story would hold up and she'd be acquitted. But I think now that it's hopeless . . . Sit down, Muriel." He guided her back to the chair and eased her into it, while her lips formed the words, *No, no, no,* and she kept shaking her head. Rod ignored her, sank into his chair and ran a shaking hand over his face.

"Only about half of her story is true," he said. "I can tell you the rest."

"I was sure you could," said Moyer softly. "And you're a man after all, Lindquist."

Wurdack looked at Moyer and the sneer was gone from his face.

Rod Lindquist lighted a cigarette, said, "I never thought of her as Star Osborne until she came here. That was her married name. Her maiden name was Andrea Stella Te-

138

desco, and she was once my secretary."

There was a hush in the room as Lieutenant Moyer nodded. "We knew that," he said. "It took a lot of tracing but we found it out. And also that she had worked for you. But that's all." He picked up the green box. "And then we got hold of this tonight. There were letters from you, written while you were on business trips. They didn't leave much doubt that you were thick with her. But still, we could only guess. It wasn't proof."

"Stella means Star in Latin," continued Lindquist with a visible .effort to take control of himself, "and I suppose that's how she got the name. I know she had an Ohio driver's license and other identification under Star Osborne because once I came across them in a desk drawer in her apartment. She knew that my wife would recognize the name Andrea Tedesco. Because when she was my secretary for a short time Muriel had talked to her on the phone, though she never met her.

"It wasn't until after she was dead that Muriel told me she had seen Andrea once before. Andrea was pointed out to her by a private detective. But Muriel was some distance away and Andrea had black hair then—dyed black and worn on top of her head in a chignon. She was forever changing her appearance and by the time she came here, her hair was back to its natural color. Muriel never recognized her, but all along she had it in the back of her mind that there was something familiar about her. She had an unreasonably strong antagonism for Andrea from the beginning."

"Come on," said Wurdack. "Get on with it!"

Lindquist didn't even turn his head. He spoke directly to Moyer. "I had been, well . . ." he smiled sadly at Muriel, "involved with Andrea for some time in San Francisco. I didn't love her—at least not the way I love Muriel. But just the same, she . . . she had a hold on me worse than heroin and I . . . I had to have her. I supported her, gave her lots of presents—and money, too. At first that was all she seemed to require. Then she began to needle me to get a divorce and marry her. I didn't want to do that. I didn't ever want to do that. But she kept at me, she never dropped the subject.

"And then when I told her foolishly that I was coming here with Muriel, and that I was in some doubt if we should continue the relationship, we had a bad fight. She made all

139

kinds of threats. I thought I had pacified her by telling her we'd work something out when I returned. But we hadn't been here a day or two when she arrived on the scene suddenly and took that little room where Erickson stays. Later she moved to the front apartment.

"Naturally, when I could get her alone, I begged her to leave. She said she would leave, all right—but with me. And only after I had promised to separate from my wife and marry her. I told her I would think about it, but that was a stall. I only loved her in one way, if you can call it love. And I'm sure if I had married her, she would have bled me and gone on to someone else. She never was anything but money-mad.

"In a few days she got me alone again and said if I didn't leave with her immediately, she was going to sleep with every man in the building. I didn't really think she meant it and I told her to go right ahead. She . . . she began with Royce here. And she carried out her threat.

"She must have known, but I had no idea how that would effect me. Slowly but surely I began literally to lose my mind. I kept it covered but inside I was twisted in knots, totally consumed with jealousy. I never slept. I was tortured with images of her like an animal with those men . . . I loathed her and yet I wanted her more than ever. The few times I could speak to her, it was useless. She just laughed at me.

"Then—on the night of the party—she said that if I didn't · agree to marry her, she was going to tell Muriel about us. And on top of that she was again fooling around with Humphrey and Royce. You can guess the rest. But if you want the details . . . I . . . well, Muriel and I left the party. We had an argument. I walked out.

"I was already loaded but I went to a bar near here and got just about dead drunk. The more I thought about Andrea, the more I wanted her and hated her. And at the same time was afraid of her. With every drink it grew worse. Until, I don't know . . . I just saw her dead, speared like a cruel and predatory shark. And then I would find relief. Her hold would be gone.

"Muriel told me later that while I was away, she went down and cut Andrea's hair. It happened just about the way she told you except the harpoon wasn't in the room at all. I saw the boat all broken up and the harpoon was lying there with the rest of the gear. I staggered into

140

Andrea's apartment with it. When I saw her, I thought she looked strange but I was too drunk to reason why. She wouldn't wake up, so I threw water in her face and kept shaking her until her eyes opened and she recognized me.

"I had the harpoon lying across the foot of the bed and I picked it up. She said, 'What are you doing with that thing, you poor slob. You look ridiculous.' I told her to keep her voice down. I was almost whispering and she was pretty loud. We got into another terrible argument which ended with her saying, over and over, 'Poor slob, can't leave mama and has to have baby, too. Fix your little red wagon good tomorrow.' And then she began to laugh and to tell me that she had had two men already that night and did I want to be the third. That was when I ripped the sheet off her and brought the harpoon up and she said something, pleading, and I drove it into her with all my might."

Lindquist held his head in his hands and said through his fingers in a choked voice, "Muriel heard some of it and guessed. She saw me come out of the apartment and up the stairs. She was so kind to me and . . . and I broke down and told her. She got up the plan to . . . to keep the hair and hide it. Then if the police found out about Andrea and me, if they had enough to arrest me, she would confess that she did it in self-defense. If she could produce the hair, well, that would be more convincing . . ."

He broke off and doubled over, moaning.

Muriel came over and knelt down and put her arms around him. She held his head against her breasts. She rocked him back and forth and there was the sound of his weeping in the silent room.

Royce got up and went to a window and held his ears to shut the agony from sight and hearing. When he turned, only Wurdack had moved. He came across the room and separated them, though with gentle hands. His voice was soft when he said, "You'd better get dressed now, Lindquist."

When Rod Lindquist stood, he was composed. He went almost to the bedroom door, then turned to look at Muriel. It was a long look and she got up slowly, then ran to him. They embraced. He kissed her. "I love you, Muriel," he said. "I've never loved anyone else."

Royce saw Wurdack look down at his toes and Moyer turned his back. Then Rod broke away from her and disappeared behind the bedroom door. Muriel returned, col-

141

lapsed in her chair, crying.

Wurdack moved toward the bedroom. Moyer shook his head. "It's a two-story drop and the detail is spread around the building," he said.

Royce crossed to Muriel, leaned over and put his arm around her. He didn't know what to say. She found his hand and squeezed it until the bones ached.

It was as Royce was looking up into the deep-sad eyes of Moyer that the sound came—like the snap of a heavy whip, lashing once with a mute distant echoing.

Moyer's head jerked toward the sound. He and Wurdack began to run toward the bedroom at the same instant.

Muriel's face lifted and she froze. Awareness sneaked into her eyes and her chin began to tremble. "What was that?" she said. "Why are they running? Why!"

She tried to get up but Royce held her fast. "Please!" she cried. "Please, please, tell me. What is it!" There was only silence from the other room.

Royce swallowed. "Muriel," he said, "did Rod have a gun?"

Her face drained, nails dug into his flesh. Then she shoved him mightily and broke away, running.

Moyer caught her at the door and held her. "Rod!" she screamed. "Rod! Rod!"

Moyer looked down into her face and shook his head. "My dear," he said. "I'm sorry. I'm terribly sorry . . ."

ten

Royce stepped around the car and lifted the lid of the trunk. He placed Laura Bishop's bag on top of his own. She came down the steps, her dark hair loose and swaying across her back. She wore a white silk blouse and aqua skirt. Her eyes were a little grave but the smile that touched her face was quietly happy.

The sun was hot in a washed-blue sky. The sea was solid green ice that darkened as it spread away to the horizon. It was noon of the following day in the last of August.

"Is that it?" Royce called. "Anything else?"

She shook her head. "Just me," she said.

142

Royce closed the lid and walked to meet her. She moved toward the patio and stood looking around her. He followed. A small frown creased her brow as her eyes walked up to the Lindquist apartment. "What happened to poor Muriel?" she asked.

"Gone," he said. "Early this morning. She wouldn't leave him. She went with the body. Moyer said he would look out for her and there was nothing I could do to help."

"Muriel, Muriel," murmured Laura. "Lost. So many people are lost, Stan. Especially the living."

Royce opened his mouth to comment but the door to Humphrey's apartment banged and he and Erickson came down the stairs in bathing trunks. Erickson paused at the bottom when he saw Royce. His face was pained, searching for words. "Thanks, Stan," he said. "I won't forget." Humphrey just smiled and waved, then they both ran apace to the water and dove in.

"Don't they care?" said Laura. "All this . . . this horror and there they go swimming as if nothing had happened."

"Of course they care," said Royce. "But on the surface they play together at forgetting. They run and they swim but somehow they don't look the same to me. Not much heart and no competition."

"But together," said Laura. "Will they stay in this awful place—now?"

"No," said Royce. "They're already packed. This is their last swim."

She turned and they walked to the car and got in. "Well," she said, "which way now? I don't have a home."

"Sure you do," said Royce. "Up in the Hollywood Hills where I live I'll find you a home so close you can lean out the window and shout to me." He took her hand and squeezed. "You won't be alone, Laura."

She looked away. "Don't say things like that, Stan. Or I'll cry. And really, I'm quite happy. Really, I am."

Royce flipped the key and the motor hummed. "As soon as we leave The Tides behind you, you'll be amazed at how happy you are," he said. He dropped the gear arm in drive and gave a last look to the building.

"My third summer here," he said. "And my last. I wonder where we'll be next August, Laura."

Laura turned to look at him and could only smile.

He nudged onto the highway, then stomped down hard on the accelerator.

143

In an hour, Humphrey and Erickson had gone and The Pacific Tides lay empty. In the late afternoon a pair of eight-year-old boys passing on the beach spied the shambles of the little green boat and paused to inspect it curiously. They climbed into it, playing with the broken steering wheel, puffing their cheeks and making busy motor-sounds, leaning into a dream wind as they were hurled forward at a dream speed of ninety miles an hour. They soon lost interest and, taking the bent wheel with them, departed.

Night came and the enormous glass eyes of the building were dark and staring. Above, in the hills of Malibu, warm lights clustered together and looked down upon the one cold patch of structural darkness along the near coast. Cars, motorcycles, buses, trucks roared, throbbed and droned past. Toward Oxnard, Ventura, Santa Barbara, San Francisco. Toward Santa Monica, Long Beach, Laguna, and San Diego. While few of the itinerant travelers knew that Malibu, small in physical stature, large in fame, had come and gone. Yet knowing of movie stars, heavenly stars, gold stars and—for three days—of Star Osborne.

But though her name and the name of Rod Lindquist got lost with the rest of yesterday's news in the trash cans of the nation, a taint of evil clung to the name Pacific Tides. Except for a lone couple who remained one week on a dare, it sat empty until the following summer when it was bought for a third of its value. Then repainted and redecorated, a wing added. Finally the name itself changed. After which it enjoyed a small success but, at last, failed.

Then a fire of mysterious origin burned it to near rubble. And a restaurant grew up on the site. The owner was Greek, a naïve little man who, over the years, had made a small fortune with a trio of hamburger stands in Buffalo, New York. He was much impressed with his surroundings, the magic of Malibu. He was awed by the proximity of The Colony and all the vast convolutions of the movie world. Unwittingly, in tall letters of blazing red neon, he crowned the restaurant—Star's Haven.

www.ingramcontent.com/pod-product-compliance
Lightning Source LLC
Chambersburg PA
CBHW010642100726
47900CB00011B/2934